Death in Venice

Thomas Mann

Table of Contents

Chapter I

Gustav Aschenbach, or *von* Aschenbach, as his official surname had been since his fiftieth birthday, had taken another solitary walk from his apartment in Munich's Prinzregentenstraße on a spring afternoon of the year 19.., which had shown the continent such a menacing grimace for a few months. Overexcited by the dangerous and difficult work of that morning that demanded a maximum of caution, discretion, of forcefulness and exactitude of will, the writer had been unable, even after lunch, to stop the continued revolution of that innermost productive drive of his, that *motus animi continuus*, which after Cicero is the heart of eloquence, and had been thwarted trying to find that soothing slumber which he, in view of his declining resistance, needed so dearly. Therefore he had gone outside soon after tea, hoping that fresh air and exertion would regenerate him and reward him with a productive evening.

It was early May, and, after some cold and wet weeks, a faux midsummer had begun. The *Englische Garten*, although only slightly leafy, was humid as in August and had been teeming with carriages and strollers where it was close to the city. At the *Aumeister*, where increasingly serene paths had led him, he had surveyed the popular and lively *Wirtsgarten*, on the bounds of which some cabs and carriages were parking, he had started his saunter home across the fields outside of the park while the light was fading, and waited, since he felt exhausted and a thunderstorm seemed imminent over Föhring, for the tram which was to carry him in a straight line back to the city. He happened to find the station and its surroundings completely deserted. Neither on the paved Ungererstraße, on which the lonely-glistening rails stretched towards Schwabing, nor on the Föhringer Chaussee a cart could be seen; nothing stirred behind the fences of the stonecutters, where crosses, commemorative plates, and monuments for sale formed a second, uninhabited cemetery and the Byzantine edifice of the mortuary chapel on the other side of the street lay silent in the last light of the parting day. Its front wall, decorated with Greek crosses and emblems in bright colors, furthermore sports symmetrically aligned biblical inscriptions concerning the afterlife, such as: "THEY ENTER THE HOUSE OF GOD" or "THE ETERNAL LIGHT MAY SHINE UPON THEM"; and the waiter for a time had found a reasonable entertainment in reading the phrases and letting his mind's eye wander in their iridescent mystery, when he, returning from his reverie, had noticed a man in the portico, close to the apocalyptic beasts which guard the staircase, whose wholly unusual appearance steered his thoughts into a completely different direction.

Whether he had emerged from inside of the hall through the bronze gates or had approached undetected from outside remained an enigma. Aschenbach, without giving particularly deep thought to the question, tended to assume the former. Not very tall, thin, beardless and strikingly round-nosed, the man belonged to the red-headed type and had its milk-like and freckled skin. Obviously he was not Bavarian: the broad and straight-rimmed bast hat which covered his head gave him the air of the foreign and far-traveled. Of course he wore the common kind of rucksack strapped on his shoulders, a yellowish suit of loden fabric, as it appeared, a gray coat over the left underarm, which he had stemmed into his side, and in the right hand a stick with an iron tip, which he had pushed diagonally into the ground and on which he, feet crossed, leaned with his hip. With raised head, so that on his scrawny neck which stuck out from his sport shirt the Adam's apple projected forcefully and well-defined, he looked into the distance, with colorless, red-lashed eyes between which there were two vertical, definite furrows, which strangely complemented his short and stubby nose. His demeanor—and perhaps his elevated and elevating standpoint contributed to this impression—was that of cool survey, audacious, even wild; because, be it that he was grimacing against the brightness of the setting Sun or that it was a more permanent physiognomic disfigurement, his lips seemed too short, the teeth were entirely uncovered, so that they, quite long and bare to the gums, gleamed white between his lips.

Possibly Aschenbach had not exerted much discretion in his half-distracted and half-inquisitive study of the foreigner; because suddenly he noticed the other one returning his glances and in such a war-like fashion, so straight into the eye, so obviously determined to carry this to the extremes and to force the other one's gaze to retreat, that Aschenbach, slightly embarrassed, turned around and began ambling along the fences, with the passing decision not to regard that person again. He had forgotten him the very next minute. If it was the wayfarer-like air of the foreigner working on his imagination or some other corporeal or mental influence that caused it: a strange distention of his soul unexpectedly made itself known, a sort of roving unrest, a juvenile thirst for the distant, a feeling, so novel and yet so long-forgotten that he, hands on his back and his eyes fixed at the ground, stood transfixed to probe that emotion and its nature and aim. It was wanderlust, nothing more; but verily coming in the form of a fit and ardently intensified, even to the point of an illusion. Because he saw, as a sample of of all those wonders and horrors of the diversity on Earth which his desire was suddenly able to imagine, an enormous landscape, a tropical swamp under a moist and heavy sky, wet, lush, and unhealthy, a primordial wilderness of islands and mud-bearing backwaters that men avoid. The shallow islands, the soil of which was covered with leafs as thick as hands, with enormous ferns, with juicy, macerated and wonderfully flowering plants, ejected upwards hairy palm trunks, and strangely formless trees, whose roots sprung from the trunks and connected to the water or the ground through the air, formed disorienting arrangements. On the brackish, glaucously-reflecting stream milk-white, bowl-sized flowers were floating; high-shouldered birds of all kinds with shapeless beaks were standing on tall legs in the shallow water and looked askance unmoving, while through vast reed fields there sounded a clattering grinding and whirring, as if by soldiers in their armaments; the onlooker thought he felt the tepid and mephitic odor of that unrestrained and unfit wasteland, which seemed to hover in a limbo between creation and decay, between the knotty trunks of a bamboo thicket he for a moment believed to perceive the phosphorescent eyes of the tiger—and felt his heart beating with horror and mysterious yearning. Finally the hallucination vanished, and Aschenbach, shaking his head, resumed his promenade along the fences of the stonecutters.

He had, as far as he had possessed the means to enjoy the benefits of sojourn to far-off countries, regarded travel as a

7

hygienic necessity, which had to be observed against will and inclination. Too much occupied with the duties imposed by his ego and the European soul, too overburdened with the duty of production, too little interested in distracting himself to be a faithful lover of that gay outside world, he had contended himself wholly with that knowledge of the Earth's surface that can be gained by anyone without ever having to abandon his circle and was never even tempted to leave Europe. The more so since his life was approaching its conclusion, since his artist's fright of not being able to finish his work, that fret that his time had run out, could no longer be called purely a delusion, so that his life had mostly been limited to the beautiful city, which had become a home to him, and the spartan country house, which he had erected in the mountains and where he spent rain-soaked summers.

Also that which had of late so suddenly touched him was soon tempered and corrected by the reason and restraint that he had exercised from his younger years on. He had intended to continue the work for which he lived up a certain point before he moved to the country and the thought of an aimless wandering around the world, which would cost him several months of time allotted for his work, seemed too carefree and at odds with his plans, it was not to be considered in earnest. And yet he was quite aware what was the cause of that affliction. It was a desire to flee, he had to admit to himself, this yearning for the distant and the novel, this desire for liberty, for being free of burden, for being able to forget—the desire to escape his work, the commonplace location of a rigorous, frigid, and ardent duty. Although he loved it and also almost the unnerving, daily-repeating struggle between his tenacious and proud, so often tested willpower and that growing weariness, of which nobody was

8

allowed to know and which was not allowed to betray the product by any sign of impotence or defeat. But it seemed reasonable not to overdo it and not to suffocate such a lively desire hardheadedly. He thought of his work, thought of the point at which he had to terminate his effort today, just like yesterday, and which seemed to yield neither to patient care nor a decisive blow. He inspected it again, tried to break or dissolve the stoppage but aborted his attack with a feeling of disgust. These were no insurmountable hindrances, what immobilized him were the scruples of listlessness, which masqueraded as an insatiable discontent. Discontent had already been considered by the adolescent as the character and innermost nature of genius and he had sought to restrain his emotions because he had realized that they are too easily contented with approximations and half-hearted perfection. Was that repressed sentiment now avenging itself by leaving him, by refusing to carry his art and by taking away all his delight with form and meaning? Not that he produced bad art: That was one of the advantages of his age, that he could be sure of his mastery in every moment. But he himself, while his nation honored it, was unable to enjoy it and it seemed to him as if his work lacked those characteristics of fiery inventiveness which, as creations of joy, contribute more to the pleasure of the readership than some inner meaning. He was afraid of the summer in the countryside, alone in that little house with the maidservant who prepared the food for him and the manservant who served it; he feared the familiar sight of the mountains and steep cliffs that would surround his listless dullness. And so there was a need for something different, some living without a set plan, some fresh air from remote places, an infusion of fresh blood to make the summer more tolerable and productive. So travel it would be—he was content with himself. Not that far, certainly not to the tigers. A night in the sleeping car and a siesta of three or four weeks in one of the usual places for holidays in the lovely South…

So he thought to himself while the noise of the electric tram approached along the Ungererstraße and when he got in he decided to spend the evening with the study of maps and schedules. On the platform it occurred to him to look for the man with the bast hat, his comrade during that rather fateful stay. But the man's whereabouts remained unknown, as he was neither to be found in his former location, nor at the next station, nor in the car.

Chapter II

The author of the articulate and powerful epic prose poem about the life of Frederick the Great; the patient artist, who had industriously weaved the tapestry called "Maja", a novel rich in characters that combined so much human fatefulness under the overruling shadow of an idea; the creator of that mighty narrative titled "A Miserable One" that demonstrated to a thankful generation the possibility of moral resoluteness in the presence of deepest knowledge; the writer, finally, (and that concludes the list of works of his most mature period) of the impassioned treatise about "Arts and the Intellect", which due to its organizing force and antithetical eloquence could be compared to Schiller's reasoning about naive and sentimental poetry: Gustav Aschenbach had been born as the son of judicial officer in the district town of L. in Silesia. His ancestors had been officers, judges, and bureaucrats, men who in the service of king and country had led their strict and decently simple lives. Intellectual tendencies had once taken shape among them in the form of a preacher; quicker, more sensual blood had been added through the poet's mother, daughter of a Bohemian bandmaster. From her the characteristics of a different race in his appearance had been derived. That marriage between businesslike, spartan sedulity and darker, more fiery impulses had created *an* artist, and *this* artist in particular. Since his entire persona had a disposition towards fame, he, even though not really precocious, had presented himself from an early age on with maturity and skill, thanks to his decisiveness and laconic use of words. Still little more than a student, he had already made a name for himself. Ten years later he had learned to represent from his desk, to administrate his fame in concise letters (because the one who is successful and trustworthy is met with many demands every day), and to be generally benevolent and meaningful. Even in his forties he had had, already exhausted from the strains and vicissitudes of his actual work, to cope with a daily correspondence bearing postage stamps from all over the world.

Keeping equal distance from the banal and the eccentric, his gifts were made to win the fidelity of the masses and the adulating, demanding participation of the more discriminating at the same time. In that way, from his adolescent years having been prepared for extraordinary achievement from all sides, he had never known the idleness and carelessness of youth. When he fell sick in Vienna around his thirty-fifth year, are careful observer said of him: "See, Aschenbach has always lived like this"—and he formed a fist with his left hand—"but never like that"—and he let his now-open hand drop nonchalantly from the armrest of his lounge chair. That was indeed true; and the brave thing about it was that his nature was not at all robust and had been made to yield to frequent concentrated effort only by calling, not by birth.

The doctor had demanded that the boy stay home from school and instead advised that he be schooled at home. He had grown up solitary, without comrades and had to recognize in due time that he belonged to a family in which not so much the talent but the necessary physical basis which talent needs to unfold had been a rarity—a family in which the capable gave all their gifts early on and infrequently reached old age. But his favorite phrase was "keep a stiff upper lip"—in his novel about Frederick the Great he saw nothing less than the apotheosis of that command, which he considered the essence of virtue at work. He also wished mostly dearly to live a long life, because he had always though that an artist could only be considered truly great and honorable if he had been a success in *all* stages of his life.

Therefore, since he had to carry the duties which his gifts burdened him with on tender shoulders and intended to go a long way, discipline was most important to him— fortunately, that kind of discipline had been running in his father's side of the family. At forty or fifty years, at an age when others are still wasteful and enthusiastic and delay the carrying out of bigger designs, he started his day by dousing his breast and back with cold water and then sacrificed the creative impulses he had gathered during his slumber during two or three hours of intensive work in the candlelight. It was pardonable, and even signified the victory of his morality when those without more intimate knowledge considered the world of "Maja" or the epic construct in which Frederick's heroic life found its expression products of an enduring force, while in reality they had been built up in tiny daily portions from hundreds of inspirations, and when they only reached a certain degree of excellence because their master had endured the imposition of a certain work for years with the same tenacity and willpower that had helped conquer his home province and had only invested his most powerful and noble hours into their creation.

For an important intellectual product to be immediately weighty, a deep relationship or concordance has to exist between the life of its creator and the general lives of the people. These people are generally unaware why exactly they praise a certain work of art. Far from being truly knowledgeable, they perceive it to have a hundred different benefits to justify their adulation; but the real underlying reason for their behavior cannot be measured, is sympathy. Aschenbach had once mentioned it in a place where it might easily have been overlooked, that all truly great works exist despite of things, despite distress and pain, despite poverty, abandonment, weakness of the body, vice, passion, and a thousand obstacles. But it was more than just a remark, it was an experience, was almost the formula of his life and fame, the key to his work; and so it was not surprising if this was also the moral disposition, the demeanor of his most memorable characters.

About that novel, always recurring kind of heroic type so favored by this writer, a keen essayist had remarked once: that he was the conception of "an intellectual and ephebe-like masculinity that stands silent in proud shame, clenching its teeth while it is pierced by swords and spears." That was beautiful, intelligent, and correct, despite its somewhat exaggerated accentuation of passivity. Because grace under pressure is more than just suffering; it is an active achievement, a positive triumph and the figure of St Sebastian is its best symbol, if perhaps not in art generally, but certainly in the art of writing. Gazing at the written world, seeing the elegant self-restraint that guards an inner decomposition, a biological decay until the last moment from the prying eyes of the world; that bilious, sensually disadvantaged ugliness that is able to kindle its smoldering fire into a pure flame and to even usurp the throne in the kingdom of beauty; the pallid impotence, which retrieves from the glowing depths of the soul the power to prostrate an entire wanton people before the cross, before *its own* feet; the amiable attitude in the empty and severe employ of the form; the counterfeit and dangerous life; the quickly unnerving yearning and art of the born fraud: considering all these things and so many others more, one could doubt if there even was a sort of heroism *not* marked by meekness. And what kind of heroism would be more timely than this one? Gustav Aschenbach was the poet of all those who were laboring on the brink of exhaustion, the overburdened and worn out, who still tried to keep upright, those moralists of performance, who, being lanky and of limited means, through willpower and clever management can conjure the effect of greatness at least for a time. They are numerous, they are the heroes of our age. And they all recognized themselves in his work, they found themselves vindicated, elevated, celebrated in it, thanked him generously and spread his name.

He was young and had been rough with time, listening to its bad advice he had made mistakes, had compromised himself, had trespassed against good behavior and prudence, both in his words and works. But he had gained that dignity towards which every genius has an inner drive, one could even say that his whole development had been a conscious and defiant ascent towards dignity, an ascent that defied all those hindrances of doubt and irony.

Lively, yet non-binding concreteness of formation is the foundation of the delight of the bourgeois masses, but the absolute ardor of youth is only interested in the problematic: and Aschenbach was problematic, had been as absolute as any other youth. He had indulged in the mind, ruthlessly mined for knowledge, had milled his seeds, given away secrets, brought talent under suspicion, betrayed art—and while his creations were entertaining and reviving and elevating the pious epicures, he, the young artist, had kept the twenty-year-olds breathless with his cynicism about the questionable nature of art and artists.

But it seems as if nothing dulls the noble and able mind quicker than the biting and bitter taste of awareness; and it is certain that the melancholy sedulous thoroughness of the youth is nothing in comparison to the deep conviction of the man who has become a master, his decision to deny that knowledge, to decline it, to completely ignore it when he finds it in the least capable of paralyzing, discouraging, and degrading. How else could the famous story of the "Miserable" be interpreted than as an outburst of disgust against the indecent psychologizing of the time, made flesh and blood in the figure of that soft and ridiculous scoundrel, who tries to trick fate by sending his wife, perhaps out of profligacy, out of moral weakness into the arms of a beardless one and thinks he is entitled to commit indecencies? The power of the word, with which the cast away is cast away, pronounces the turning away from all moral uncertainty, from every sympathy with the abyss, the reneging of that phrase of compassion, that "to understand all is to forgive all", and what was beginning here was that "wonder of the reborn impartiality", which was briefly mentioned in one of the author's dialogues with not a little mystery. What strange coherence! Was it a consequence of that "rebirth", that newfound dignity and severity, that at the same time an almost extreme enhancement of his sense of beauty was observed, that kind of noble purity, simplicity, and well-proportionedness of form, which from then on gave his works such a deliberate air of mastery and classicism? But moral determination without knowledge, without that dissolving and hindering perception—does it not also entail a simplification, a moral black-and-white view of the world and the soul and therefore also a tendency towards what is evil and forbidden? And is not form itself two-faced? Is it not moral and amoral at the same time—moral as an expression of discipline, amoral and even antimoral if it encompasses a moral indifference and tries to rule over what is moral?

However it may be! Development is also fate; and why should not the one which is participated in by the public take a different course from that which unfolds without the glamor and the duties of fame? Only never-ending vagary finds it boring and is wont to ridicule it when a remarkable talent outgrows its libertine past, gets used to expressly perceive the dignity of the mind and takes on the solitary mores full of unadvised, hardly independent sorrows and struggles which ascend to power and honors among men. Besides, how much play, resentment, indulgence is in the remaking of talent by itself! An official and paedagogic element slowly surfaced in Gustav Aschenbach's performances, his style departed from the direct boldness, those subtle and new distinctions of his earlier years, it transformed itself into the exemplary and solid, the conventionally polished, the preserving, formal, even formulaic, and like the anecdote about the Sun King purports to know, so the aging one exiled every base and common word from his vocabulary: At that time it happened that the ministry of education included selected writings of his in their schoolbooks. It suited him very well, and he did not resent it all when a German prince, just recently crowned, knighted the creator of the "Frederick" on his fiftieth birthday.

After several years of unrest and much trying out of different places he soon picked Munich as his permanent hometown and there he lived in those bourgeois honors that in rare cases are bestowed upon the intellect. His marriage to a girl, the offspring of a highly educated family, had been terminated by her death. A daughter, already married herself, had remained. He had never had a son.

Gustav von Aschenbach was not particularly tall, with dark hair, beardless. His head seemed curiously oversized in relation to his almost frail figure. His brushed-back hair, thinning at the cortex, very voluminous at the temples and quite gray, framed a high, furrowed and, so to say, scarred forehead. The frame of golden eyeglasses cut into the root of a somewhat plump yet nobly curved nose. His mouth was large, often limp, sometimes small and tense all of a sudden; his cheeks were narrow and furrowed, the well-formed chin sported a cleft. Important fates seemed to have trespassed over the often sideways-tilted crown, and yet it had been art which had shaped that kind of physiognomy which otherwise is the hallmark of a difficult and troubled life. Behind that brow, the glittering repartees in the conversation between the King and Voltaire about war had been born; these eyes, looking at the world wearily through the glasses, had seen the bloody inferno in the field hospitals of the Seven Years' War. Even on a personal level art is a form of heightened living. It gives greater pleasures, it consumes faster. It stamps the features of its servants with the signs of imaginary and spiritual adventures, and it produces, even in the most cloister-like atmosphere, a certain fastidiousness, an over-refinement, an exhaustion and curiosity of the nerves, in a way even a life of the most outrageous passions and delights could scarcely effect it.

Chapter III

Some business of the worldly and literary kind held the hopeful traveler-to-be back in Munich for another two weeks after that walk. Finally he gave orders to prepare his country house for him within four weeks and then one day between the middle and the end of May he took the night train to Trieste, where he only stopped for twenty-four hours and the next day embarked for Pola. What he was looking for was the unfamiliar and unrelated, which was indeed reached rather easily and so he stayed on a celebrated Adriatic island, situated not far from the Istrian coast, with a gaily ragged people that conversed in an alien-sounding language and with picturesquely broken cliffs where the sea was open. Unfortunately, heavy rain and an oppressive atmosphere, a parochial and completely Austrian company in the hotel and the lack of calm and easy communion with the sea which only a soft-sloping and sandy beach can afford, caused him distress, prevented in him the feeling that he had reached his destination; an innermost calling of his, he did not know to where, caused him alarm, he studied the passenger ship routes, he looked around searchingly, and all of a sudden, at the same time surprising and expected, his destination became clear to him. When one wanted to see something without equal, the romantically different, where would one go? There could be no question about it. What was he supposed to do *here*? He had erred. He should have had traveled to that other location in the first place. He did not hesitate to immediately cancel his abortive stay on the island. One-and-a-half weeks after his arrival on the island, at hazy dawn a fast launch took him and his luggage back to the military harbor and there he only went ashore to directly step onto the damp deck of a ship bound for Venice.

It was a vehicle under an Italian flag, stricken with years, outmoded, serene, and somber. In a cave-like, artificially-lit berth, into which Aschenbach had been instantly ushered with grinning courtesy by a humpbacked and dirty sailor after setting foot onto the ship, there sat a behind a table with his hat slanted on his head and with a cigarette butt between his lips a goatish man who had the physiognomy of an old-fashioned circus director, who with artificially easy demeanor registered the nationalities of the travelers and handed them their tickets. "To Venice!" he repeated Aschenbach's request, straightening his arm and pushing the quill into the pulpy remains of an inclined inkstand. "First class to Venice! Here you are, sir!" And he wrote with huge loops, dispensed some blue sand from a can onto the writing, let the sand run into a clay bowl, folded the paper with yellow and bony fingers and continued his writing. "A happily chosen destination!" he chattered meanwhile. "Ah, Venice! A magnificent city! A city full of irresistible attraction to the well-educated, both due to its history and its present charms!" The smooth dispatch of his movements and the empty talk that accompanied them had something stupefying and distracting, almost as if he feared the passenger might waver in his determination to go to Venice. He speedily cashed the money and let the change fall onto the dirty tablecloth with the dexterity of a croupier. "Have a nice day, sir!" he said with a thespian bow. "It is my honor to convey you… Next please!" he cried with a raised arm, pretending his business was lively even though there was nobody else around who needed a ticket. Aschenbach returned onto the deck.

Leaning with one arm on the handrail, he contemplated both the idle people who were mooching at the pier to witness the ship's departure and his fellow passengers. Those of the second class were crouching on the foredeck, using boxes and bundles as seats. A group of young people formed the company of the first deck, apparently tradesman's apprentices from Pola who had merrily united for a trip to Italy. They made a lot of fuss about themselves and their enterprise, chattered, laughed, contentedly enjoyed their own gesticulating and mocked those colleagues, who, portfolios tucked under their arms, were walking along the street to pursue their business and who made threatening gestures to the departing. One in a bright yellow, excessively fashionable summer suit, red tie, and a boldly bent up panama hat, exceeded all the others with his shrill voice and gayness. No sooner had Aschenbach set eyes on him than he realized with a kind of terror that this ephebe was false. He was ancient, there could be no doubt about it. Wrinkles surrounded his mouth and eyes. The meek crimson of his cheeks was makeup, that brown hair below the colorfully-banded straw hat was a wig, his neck was dilapidated and sinewy, his moustache was dyed, his yellowish and complete set of teeth which he laughingly presented was a cheap counterfeit, and his hands with signet rings on both index fingers were that of a very old man. With a shudder Aschenbach looked at him and his communion with his friends. Did they not know or notice they he was elderly, that he was wrongfully appropriating their garish dress, fraudulently played one of theirs? As if nothing had happened, seemingly out of habit, they tolerated him among

21

themselves, treated him as an equal, answered his teasing nudges without disgust. How could that be? Aschenbach covered his forehead with his hand and closed his eyes that were burning from a lack of sleep. He felt as if reality was becoming unreal, as if a dreamlike enchantment had begun, a shift of the world into the inexplicable, which perhaps could be opposed by closing his eyes and then taking another look. But in that moment he became aware of a sensation of floating and strangely startled he realized that the heavy and dark mass of the ship had detached itself from the quay. Inch by inch, with the engine running alternately forwards and backwards, the strip of dirtily iridescent water between the ship's hull and the shore widened, and after some stodgy maneuvers, the steamer's bow was pointing towards the open sea. Aschenbach went over the the starboard side, where the humpbacked sailor had prepared a deck chair for him and a steward in a spotted dress coat awaited his orders.

The sky was gray, the wind moist; the harbor and the islands had receded, and soon land was no longer visible. A snow of coal dust, soaked with humidity, settled on the freshly-scrubbed deck that refused to dry. After about an hour the tent roof was deployed, as it had begun to rain.

Wrapped in his coat, a book in his lap, the traveler rested and time seemed to fly. The rain had ceased; the linen roof was removed. The horizon was complete. Beneath the broad cupola of the sky the enormous disc of the barren sea extended all around; but in that empty, measureless space our sense of time also suffers, and we daze in the disorienting shapelessness. Strange and shade-like creatures, the senescent dandy, the goat-bearded man from below decks, traipsed with vague gestures and confused dream-words through the mind of the reclining artist, and eventually he fell asleep.

At noon he was required to venture below into the corridor-like dining hall, which was bordered on by the sleeping bunks, eating the ordered meal at a long table, on the other side of which the apprentices, including the senex, had been drinking heavily with the jolly captain since ten o'clock. The meal was meager and he quickly finished it. He wanted to go outside, to look at the sky: if maybe it would brighten in the direction of Venice.

He did not anticipate anything else, for the city had always received him with splendor. But the sky and the sea remained cloudy and leaden, at times a fog-like drizzle fell, and slowly he accepted that he would, reaching it by water, discover a vastly different Venice from that which he had approached over land. He stood next to the foremast, gazing into the distance, expecting to see land. He thought of that melancholy-enthusiastic poet who had met the cupolas and bell towers of his dreams in this place, he quietly recalled some of the products of that awe-stricken, happy, and sad mood and moved by that ready-made emotion he wondered whether he, although more somber and tired than then, would meet that state of rapture and confusion a second time.

Then to his right the soft-sloping shore appeared, fishing boats made the sea lively, the Lido came into view, the steamer passed it on the right, gliding slowly through the channel of the same name and close to the lagoon it came to a rest entirely in full view of the poor and gaudy houses, since the barge of the sanitary service had to be met.

An hour passed before it materialized. One had reached one's destination and yet one had not; there was no hurry and yet one soon got impatient. The youths of Pola, perhaps also drawn to the military trumpet signals that echoed over the waters, had come on deck, and, enthusiastic from the Asti they had drunken, they cheered the Bersaglieri who were being drilled there. But it was repugnant to witness the state into which his faux communion with youth had brought the overdressed old man. His old and faded brain had not been able to resist the liquor to the same degree as the real youths, he was hopelessly drunk. Looking stupidly around, a cigarette between his trembling fingers, he swayed, barely able to keep his balance, pulled to and fro by his intoxication. Because he would have fallen down at the very first step, he did not dare to move, yet still displayed a sorry cockiness, holding on to everyone who approached him, speaking with a slur, winking, giggling, raising his ringed and wrinkled index finger to tease ridiculously, and licking the corners of his mouth in the most distastefully ambiguous manner. Aschenbach watched him with an expression of anger, and again he got a feeling of unreality, as if the world showed a small but definite tendency to slip into the peculiar and grotesque; a sensation which the resumption of the pounding work of the engine kept him from exploring fully, as the ship returned to its course through the San Marco canal. So he again set eyes on the most astounding landing, that blinding composition of fantastic architecture, which the Republic has to offer the awestruck looks of the approaching seafarer: the light grandeur of the Palace and the Bridge of Sighs, the columns topped with the lion and the saint close to the shore, the flauntingly projecting flank of St Mark's, the view of St Mark's Clock, and thus contemplating he thought that arriving in Venice from the train station was like entering a palace through the servants' entrance and that one should always, like himself, travel across the ocean to the most improbable of cities.

The engine stopped, gondolas approached, the accommodation ladder was lowered, the customs officials came aboard and carried out their duty; the debarkation could begin. Aschenbach made it clear that he desired a gondola to bring him and his luggage to the landing of the smaller steamers that cruise between the city and the Lido; because he wanted a room close to the sea. His wish is approved and hollered towards the water, where the gondoliers are quarreling in dialect. He is unable to descend, as his trunk is taken with great effort down the ladder-like stairs. So he cannot get away for several minutes from the intrusiveness of the ghastly old man, who is compelled by his drunkenness to bid the foreigner good-bye. "We are wishing a most enjoyable stay. One hopes to be remembered well! *Au revoir, excusez* and *bonjour*, Your Excellency!" His mouth is watering, he winks, licks the corners of his mouth and the dyed moustache on his lips is ruffled up. "Our compliments," he continues with two fingertips at his mouth, "our compliments to your sweetheart, the most lovely and beautiful sweetheart..." And suddenly the upper row of his false teeth drops onto his tongue. Aschenbach was able to escape. "To your sweetheart, the most pretty sweetheart," he heard in hollow and somewhat obstructed speech behind his back while he descended the ladder.

Who would not have had to fight a slight unease, a secret resentment and trepidation when one, for the first or after a long time, had to get into a Venetian gondola? That strange vehicle, which seems unchanged from more fanciful times and which is so strangely black like normally only coffins are, reminds one of silent and criminal adventures in the lapping night, furthermore it is reminiscent of death itself, the bier, the drab funeral and the final, wordless ride. And has one noticed that the coffin-black-varnished, black-upholstered chair in such a barge is the softest, most luxurious, most deeply relaxing seat in the whole world? Aschenbach noticed it when he took his place at the feet of the gondolier, with his luggage orderly arranged at the front of the gondola. The rowers were still quarreling, in a raw and incomprehensible way, with menacing gestures. But the peculiar quietude of the city on the sea seemed to absorb and disembody their voices and to disperse them above the water. It was fairly hot in the harbor. Touched by the warm scirocco, seated on tender cushions, the traveler closed his eyes to enjoy that kind of unusual and sweet lassitude. The trip will be short, he thought; oh would it last forever! The noiseless rocking let him put a distance between himself and that boisterous jostle.

How it became even more still around him all the time! Nothing could be heard except the lapping of the oar, the hollow impact of the waves against the tip of the gondola, that stood erect, dark and like a spear above the water and a third thing, the whispering and murmuring of the gondolier, who was talking to himself between his clenched teeth in occasional outbursts. Aschenbach raised his head and with a slight bemusement he noticed that the lagoon around him widened and the his course was towards the open sea. Therefore it seemed he should not relax too much but instead supervise the carrying out of his orders.

—"To the steamship landing, please!" he said, turning over his shoulder. The murmuring ceased. He got no reply.

—"To the steamship landing!" he repeated and turned around completely to look up into the gondolier's face, who was standing behind him, a little elevated, in front of the pale sky. It was a man of unpleasing, even violent physiognomy, dressed in blue sailor's garb, girded with a yellow sash and with a shapeless straw hat that had begun to dissolve at its edges slanted on his head. The form of his face, his blond and curly moustache below the stubby nose did not make him look very Italian. Although of relatively slender build, so that he did not seem particularly suited to his trade, he showed great energy when he used his whole body to drive the oar at every beat. A few times the exertion caused him to withdraw his lips and expose his white teeth. With his gaze fixed above the guest and his reddish eyebrows wrinkled he replied in a determined, almost harsh tone:

—"You are going to the Lido."

Aschenbach replied:

—"Indeed. But I only wanted the gondola to take me to St Mark's Square. I wish to go with the vaporetto."

—"You cannot go with the vaporetto, sir."

—"And why not?"

—"Because the vaporetto does not transport luggage."

That was correct; Aschenbach remembered. He was silent. But the brusque, boastful, uncharacteristic behavior of that man seemed intolerable. He said:

—"That is my concern. Maybe I'd like to place my luggage in custody. You will turn around."

He remained taciturn. The oar was lapping, the water clashed dully against the bow. And the talking and murmuring resumed: the gondolier was speaking to himself between his teeth.

What had to be done? Alone on the water with the strangely disobedient, unsettlingly determined man the traveler did not see a way to force upon him his will. And how softly he could be seated if he did not protest. Had he not wished that the trip should take longer, or forever? It was most prudent to let things take their course, and besides it was most comfortable. A spell of torpidity seemed to emanate from that low and black seat, so tenderly rocked by the oar beats of the defiant gondolier in his back. The notion of having fallen into the hands of a rogue streaked dreamlike through Aschenbach's mind—unable to summon his senses for active defense. Less appetizing was the possibility that this was just an act of extortion. A certain feeling of duty, the realization that one had to guard against such a thing, allowed him to make another effort. He asked:

—"How much do you want for the fare?"

And looking above him the gondolier responded:

—"You will pay."

It was clear what had to be replied to this. Aschenbach said mechanically:

—"I will pay you nothing, nothing at all if you take me somewhere I did not want to go."

—"You want to go to the Lido."

—"But not with you."

—"I row you well."

That much is true, thought Aschenbach and relaxed again. It is true, you are rowing me well. Even if you are trying to get my money and would kill me with a quick blow of the oar, you would have rowed me well. But nothing of the sort happened. Even some company appeared, a boat with musical mendicants, men and women, singing to the accompaniment of guitars and mandolins, coming obtrusively close to the gondola, filling the quietude above the waters with their mercenary tunes. Aschenbach threw a few coins into the hat that was presented. They fell silent and rowed away. And the murmuring of the gondolier was perceptible once more.

And so one arrived, rocked by the backwash of a steamer headed for the city. Two municipal officers, hands clasped behind their backs, their heads facing the lagoon, were walking back and forth at the shore. Aschenbach got off the gondola at the pier, with help from the old man with his grappling hook who seems to be present on all Venetian landings; and because he did not have enough coins he entered the hotel which was situated across from the landing, to exchange some money and reward the gondolier as he pleased. He is served in the lobby, he returns, find his luggage on a cart at the quay, and the gondola and gondolier have disappeared.

—"He has taken off," said the old man with the grappling hook. "A very bad man, a man without a license, dear sir. He is the only gondolier without a license. The others have telephoned here. He saw that he was being expected. So he took off."

Aschenbach shrugged his shoulders.

—"The sir has had a free ride," said the old man and presented his hat. Aschenbach threw in some coins. He gave orders to take his luggage to the Hotel des Bains and followed the cart through the alleyway, that white-blossoming alley, which, bordered by taverns, bazaars, and bed and breakfasts, runs across the island to the beach.

He entered the sprawling hotel from the rear, from the garden terrace and went through the lobby to the office. Because he had been announced, he was greeted with servile complicity. A manager, a diminutive, soft-spoken, ingratiatingly courteous man with a black moustache and a frock coat in the French style, accompanied him in the elevator to the third floor and showed him his room, a pleasant room with cherry furniture, decorated with heavily fragrant flowers and which had tall windows affording a view of the sea. He stepped close to one of them, after the manager had taken his leave, and while behind him his luggage was carried in, he surveyed the beach which lay deserted in the afternoon and the sunless sea at high tide sending its crouched and elongated waves in a steady rhythm against the shore.

The observations and encounters of the solitary and mute one are at the same time more blurry and more distinctive than those of the more sociable person, his thoughts more substantial, stranger, and never without a trace of sadness. Images and perceptions that would be easy to dismiss with a laugh, a short exchange of words, occupy him excessively and grow deeper and more important in silence, become experience, adventure, emotion. Solitude favors the original, the daringly and otherworldly beautiful, the poem. But it also favors the wrongful, the extreme, the absurd, and the forbidden.—Thus the unusual incidences on the journey were still disconcerting to the traveler, the horrible old man with his blabbering about a sweetheart, the gondolier who had not received payment. Without obstructing reason or giving any real food for thought, they were still extremely bizarre and possibly so bewildering because of that contradiction. In between he greeted the sea with his eyes and delighted in the knowledge that Venice could be so quickly and easily reached. Finally he turned, washed his face, gave some orders to the chambermaid to improve his comfort and had the green-liveried Swiss elevator attendant take him to the ground floor.

He took his tea on the seaside terrace, then descended and walked a good distance along the shore in the direction of the Hotel Excelsior. Upon his return it appeared to be time to dress for dinner. He did that slowly and with diligence, yet found himself still too early in the dining hall, where a group of hotel guests, unknown to each other and in feigned disinterest, had congregated in the expectation of a meal. He picked up a paper, seated himself in a club chair and contemplated the company which differed in a most agreeable way from that during his earlier stay on the island.

A wide and all-encompassing horizon opened itself out. Muffled sounds from many different languages were mixing. The omnipresent dinner jacket, the uniform of the civilized world, gathered all facets of human variety into one orderly whole. One saw the dry and elongated face of the American, the large Russian family, English ladies, German children with French nannies. The Slavic component appeared to predominate. Polish was spoken right next to him.

It was a group of adolescents and bare adults, under the supervision of a governess around a small table: three young girls, perhaps between fifteen and seventeen, and a long-haired boy of about fourteen years. With astonishment Aschenbach noticed that the boy was perfectly beautiful. His countenance—pale and gracefully reserved, surrounded by honey-colored locks, with its evenly sloped nose, the lovely mouth, the expression of alluring and divine earnestness, was reminiscent of Greek statues from the most noble period, and with all its perfection of form it had such a personal appeal that the onlooker thought he had never encountered anything similar either in nature or in art. What else was striking was an apparently deliberate contrast between the educational guidelines after which the children were dressed and kept in general. The exterior of the girls, the oldest of which could be taken for an adult, was tart and chaste to the point of disfigurement. A uniform monastic garb, shale-toned, of average length, sober and consciously unbecoming, with white collars as the only bright spot, suppressed and made impossible any pleasingness of figure. The smooth hair that appeared to be glued to the head gave their faces a featurelessness and nunlike lack of expression. It seemed certain this was the work of a mother, and naturally it did not occur to her to apply that same paedagogic severity that pertained to the girls to the boy also. Mellowness and affection visibly ruled his existence. One had abstained from cutting his arresting hair; like the statue of the Boy with Thorn it curled onto the forehead, over the ears, and even more so in the nape. An English sailor suit, the voluminous sleeves of which were tapered towards the ends and which surrounded the delicate joints of his still childlike and narrow hands, contributed, with its strings, bows, and embroideries, an air of wealth and fastidiousness. He was sitting, in semiprofile from Aschenbach's point of view, one foot in front of the other, with an elbow leaning on the armrest of his basket chair, his cheek comforted by his closed hand, in an attitude of relaxed decorum and completely without the submissive stiffness that his sisters seemed to be used to. Was he sick? Because the white of his skin contrasted like ivory with the golden somberness of the adjacent curls. Or was he simply a coddled favorite child, carried by partial and capricious devotion? Aschenbach was inclined to believe that. Almost every artistic individual has a luxurious and treacherous propensity to recognize beauty-creating inequity and to render homage to aristocratic entitlement.

A waiter went around and announced the readiness of the meal in English. Slowly the society disappeared through the glass door into the dining room. Latecomers passed by, arriving from the vestibule or the elevator. Inside the serving had begun, but the young Poles remained seated around the little tables and Aschenbach, sitting snugly in his chair, not to mention having a favorable view of something beautiful, lingered along with them.

The governess, a stocky dame with a reddish face, finally gave the signal to rise. With lifted eyebrows she shoved back her chair and bowed, when a tall lady, dressed in white and gray and richly attired with pearls, entered the room. She comported herself with coolness and restraint, the arrangement of her lightly powdered hair and the style of her dress were of that simplicity which always rules good taste where devoutness is considered an element of noblesse. She could have been the wife of a high-ranking German official. Something extravagant only entered her appearance through her jewelry, which seemed extremely expensive and consisted of earrings and a triple, very long necklace of cherry-sized, mildly shimmering pearls.

The children had arisen promptly. They kissed their mother's hand, who looked above their heads with an aloof smile of her well-groomed but slightly tired and sharp-nosed face and addressed a few words in French to the governess. Then she proceeded towards the glass door. The children followed her: the girls ordered by age, then the governess, and finally the boy. For some unknown reason he turned around before crossing the threshold and since nobody else was present, his curiously dark-gray eyes met those of Aschenbach, who, with the newspaper on his lap and deep in his thoughts, had traced the group.

What he had seen was certainly not remarkable in its details. One had not gone to table before the mother, one had waited for her, greeted her and observed the usual customs on entering the dining room. But somehow all that was presented with such a deliberate accentuation of manners, commitment, and self-respect that Aschenbach felt strangely moved by it. He hesitated for a few moments and then also went into the dining room and had himself seated, unfortunately quite far from the Polish family as he observed with regret.

Exhausted and yet in mental commotion, he entertained himself with abstract, even transcendental subjects during dinner, mulled the mysterious link between the orderly and the individual for human beauty to appear, departed from there to think about the general problems of form and art and eventually found his thoughts and findings to resemble certain apparently fortuitous ideas in a dream, that on closer inspection reveal themselves to be completely stale and unworkable. After the meal he went into the park that was filled with evening smells and smoked, sometimes sitting, sometimes walking, then he went to bed even though it was still early and spent the night in sleep that was consistently deep, but enlivened by dreams of the most varied kinds.

The weather had not improved on the next day. A land breeze was stirring. Under a pale and overcast sky the sea lay in dull quietness, shrunken so to say, with a soberingly clear horizon and so far removed from the beach than it exposed several large sandbanks. When Aschenbach opened his window, he believed to sense the putrid smell of the lagoon.

Discontent befell him. Already he considered departing. Once, a few years ago, this kind of weather had, after two sunny spring weeks, struck him and had impacted his mood in such a way that he had had to flee from Venice. Did not again that febrile listlessness, that pressure in the temples, that heaviness of the eyelids make themselves known? Moving to a new lodging for another time would be tiresome; but if the wind did not change direction, he would not stay. Just in case he did not fully unpack his luggage. At nine o'clock he ate breakfast in the special room that was reserved for that use, between the lobby and the dining room.

In the buffet room that ceremonial silence reigned that is part of the ambition of every great hotel. The waiters tiptoed around while serving. A clattering of the tea service, a half-whispered word was all that could be heard. In a corner, diagonally across from the door and two tables apart from him, Aschenbach noticed the Polish girls with their governess. Very upright, the ash blond hair newly flattened and with red eyes, in stiff dresses made of blue linen with little white collars and cuffs they sat there and handed each other the jam. They had almost finished their breakfast. The boy was absent.

Aschenbach smiled to himself. "So, my little Phaeacian!" he thought. "You seem to possess the privilege of sleeping in." And suddenly merry he recited the line from a poem below his breath:

"Jewelry, a hot bath, and rest have often made a difference."

He ate without hurry, received some letters from the porter, who had come to the room with his cap taken off, and opened a few of them while smoking a cigarette. So it happened that he still witnessed the entrance of the long sleeper who was already expected at the other table.

He came in through the glass door and ambled through the silence diagonally across the room to his sisters' table. His walk was very graceful, both in his stance and in the movement of the knees, the way his feet touched the ground, very light, at the same time tender and proud and made more appealing through the childlike self-consciousness with which he looked up and down two times while crossing the room. Smiling, with a soft word in his fuzzy-sounding language he took his place, and now that he presented the onlooker with his full profile, Aschenbach was taken by surprise again, even frightened by the godlike beauty of that human child. That day the lad was wearing a light suit of blue and white fabric with a bow of red silk on his breast and a simple white collar. Above that collar, which did not even fit the rest of the suit very elegantly, the flower of his crown rested with unequaled charm—the head of Eros, with the yellowish tint of Parisian marble, with exquisite and somber brows, temples and ear covered by the dark and soft curls of his hair.

Well, well, thought Aschenbach with that cool approval of the specialist, with which artists at times cloak their transports of delight in the face of a masterwork. And further he thought: Truly, are not the sea and the beach waiting for me, I will remain here as long as you! So he went across the hall, greeted by the waiters, along the great terrace and straight over the boardwalk to the private beach reserved for hotel guests. He let the barefoot old man, who was, in his linen pants, sailor's blouse, and straw hat, working as a bath attendant there, show him his little beach hut, had a chair and table taken from inside and put in front of it on the wooden platform and made himself comfortable in the deck chair, which he had put up a bit closer to the sea in the wax-yellow sand.

The scene at the beach, that picture of carefree and sensual enjoyment next to the sea, entertained and delighted him as always. The gray and even ocean was enlivened by wading children, swimmers, garish figures, others, who were laying on sandbanks with their arms folded under their heads. Some were rowing small boats in red and blue without a keel, capsizing with roaring laughter. In front of the row of beach huts, whose platforms were like little verandas, there was playful motion and lazy rest, visits and chattering, careful early morning elegance but also nudity, which pertly took pleasure in the freedom of the place. Closer to the sea, lone figures were strolling on the moist and firm sand in white dressing gowns or in voluminous, colorful garb. An intricate sand castle to Aschenbach's right, built by children, was sporting all around tiny flags of many different countries. Vendors of mussels, pies, and fruit were on their knees spreading out their goods. On the left, in front of a hut that stood at a right angle to the other ones and was the endpoint of the beach on that side, a Russian family was camping: men with beards and large teeth, mellow and idle women, a

Baltic damsel, who was sitting in front of an easel and was painting the sea with intermittent cries of despair, two benevolent and ugly children, an old maidservant with a kerchief and tenderly servile slave manners. In grateful appreciation they were living there, always calling out the names of the unruly youngsters, jesting for a long time with the old man thanks to a few words of Italian, buying sweets, kissing each other on the cheeks, and generally not caring about any onlookers.

So I will stay, Aschenbach thought. Where could it be better? And with his hands folded in his lap he allowed his eyes to wander in the vastness of the sea, his gaze slipping, becoming blurred, and breaking in the monotonous mist of nothingness. He loved the ocean for important reasons: out of the desire for tranquility harbored by the hard-working artist, who seeks to conceal himself from the multitude of possibilities by embracing the simple and immense; out of a forbidden proclivity for the unordered, the immeasurable, the eternal, the void that was made even more attractive by running counter to his work. To find peace in the presence of the faultless is the desire of the one who seeks excellence; and is not nothingness a form of perfection? While he was dreaming into the deepness of space, he suddenly became aware of a human figure close to the shoreline and when he collected his glance from the unlimited, it turned out to be the beautiful boy, who, coming from the left, was crossing the sand before him. He was barefoot, ready for wading, his slender legs bared till above the knees, advancing slowly, but so nimbly and proudly as if he was used to walking without footwear and he surveyed the huts. No sooner had he noticed the peaceful Russian family than his face was clouded by a tempest of scorn and disdain. His brow darkened, his mouth was lifted, between the lips and the cheeks an embittered tearing took place, and his eyebrows were so heavily wrinkled that they made the eyes appear sunken in and let them speak the evil and somber language of hatred. He averted his glance, beheld them another time, made a fiercely dismissive gesture with his shoulder and turned his back unto the enemy.

A sort of tenderness or terror, something like shame or respect caused Aschenbach to turn away as if he had seen nothing; because the serious observer of a casual passion refuses to admit his impressions even to himself. But he was delighted and shocked at the same time: that is, elated. This childish fanaticism which was directed at the most benign slab of life—it made the divinely vacant a part of the human order; it made nature's precious work of art, that had only been fit to be an eyeful, seem worthy of a deeper sympathy; and it gave the already striking personage of the youth a historico-political backdrop that allowed him to be taken seriously in spite of his age.

Still turned away, Aschenbach listened to the boy's speech, his high-pitched and somewhat feeble voice, with which he tried to announce himself to his comrades playing at the sand castle. The replies consisted in calling him by his real name or a pet name and Aschenbach paid interested attention, without being able to hear them perfectly, to two melodic syllables like "Adgio" or more frequently "Adgiu" with a vocatively-stretched "oo" sound at the end. He delighted in the tone of it, he found its pleasantness befitting the thing it described, repeated it below his breath and contently moved on to his letters and other paperwork.

His little writing case on his lap, he began to pen assorted correspondence. But after about a quarter of an hour had passed, it occurred to him how unfortunate it was to let this situation, the most delightful he had known, pass by like that. He moved aside his writing utensils, returned to the sea, and after a short while, seated on his deck chair and distracted by the voices of the children who were working on the sand castle, he turned his head to the right to further investigate the comings and goings of the marvelous Adgio.

His glance immediately discovered him; the red bow on his breast was difficult to miss. Occupied with the others in furnishing an old plank as a drawbridge for the sand castle, he gave loud orders for that endeavor, emphasizing his commands with movements of his head. With him there were about ten comrades in all, boys and girls, some of his age and some younger, speaking in Polish, French, and languages of the Balkans. But it was his name that was heard most often. Obviously he was popular, courted, admired. One of them, a stocky lad who was called "Jaschu," with black, slicked-back hair and in a linen suit, appeared to be his closest servant and confidant. When the daily work on the sand edifice had finished, they ambled along the beach in each other's arms, and the one called "Jaschu" placed a kiss on the beautiful Adgio's cheek.

Aschenbach was tempted to make a threatening gesture with the finger to Jaschu. "I advise you, Critobulus," he thought smilingly, "to leave for a year! Because it will take as much time for you to recover." And then he went on to eat a breakfast of very large and ripe strawberries which he had obtained from a vendor. It had gotten very hot, although the Sun had been unable to penetrate the layer of haze in the sky. Lassitude immobilized the mind, while the senses were taking pleasure in the immense and deadening spectacle of the silent sea. To divine, to explore which name it might be that sounded a bit like "Adgio" was considered by the earnest man a fitting and absolutely filling task and occupation. With the help of some Polish remembrances he decided that it had to be "Tadzio," short for "Tadeusz" and "Tadziu" in the vocative. Tadzio was bathing. Aschenbach, who had lost him from his sight, found his head, his arm, with which he made rowing motions, far away out on the sea; because it was quite shallow for a great distance. But immediately there was concern about him, female voices were calling out for him from the huts, exclaiming again that word which was like a password at the beach and that, with its soft sound and its drawn out "oo" sound at the end, had something both sweet and wild about it: "Tadziu, Tadziu!" He obeyed, he ran through the flood, causing the water to foam with his legs, his head tilted backwards; and to witness how the lively figure, pretty and harsh in a not-yet-manly way, with dripping curls and handsome like a youthful god, ascended from the watery depths of sky and sea: That sight induced mythical connotations, he was like a poem about ancient times, the birth of form and the genesis of the gods. Aschenbach intently listened to that song that came from inside; and again he thought that it was good to be here and that he wanted to stay.

Later Tadzio lay, exhausted from his bathing, on the sand, wrapped in white linen which was tucked under the right shoulder, resting with his head on his bare arm; and even when Aschenbach was not looking at him but read a few pages in his book, he almost never forgot the recumbent and that he only had to turn his head slightly to the right to catch sight of the admirable. It almost seemed to him as if he was guarding the resting boy—occupied with his own things and yet with unwavering vigilance for that supreme specimen to his right, not far from him. And a fatherly awe, the complete devotion of the one who tries to create beauty to the one who is endowed with it filled and moved his heart.

At noon he departed from the beach, returned to the hotel, and took the elevator to his room. Inside he spent some time in front of the mirror and studied his gray hair, his weary and sharply-cut face. In that moment he thought of his fame, and how many people looked up to him for his ability to always find the right words and graceful phrases—he called to witness all the successes his gifts had given him that he could think of and even considered his knighthood. Then he went down to the dining room and took a meal at his little table. When he entered the elevator afterwards, young people jostled into that tiny hovering cubbyhole, who were also coming from breakfast, and Tadzio joined them. He stood very close to Aschenbach, for the first time close enough that Aschenbach was afforded a more intimate look with all details. Someone addressed the lad, and while he replied with an unimaginably lovely smile, he already stepped out at the second floor, walking backwards, with downcast eyes. Beauty makes one shy, thought Aschenbach and mulled why this would be the case. He had in fact noticed that Tadzio's teeth were not quite as pleasant; slightly jagged and pale, without the sheen of health and of a strangely translucent quality as in someone with anemia. He is a bit frail, he is sickly, thought Aschenbach. He will probably not live very long. And he declined to account for the feeling of satisfaction and calmness that accompanied that notion.

He spent two hours in his room and took the vaporetto across the foul-smelling lagoon to Venice in the afternoon. He got out at St Mark's Square, took his tea there and then commenced a walk through the city, according to his local schedule. But it was this walk which caused a total reversal in his mood and his decisions.

A revolting sultriness could be felt in the alleys, the air was so heavy that the odors that emanated from the apartments, stores, and cookshops, like those of hot oil, clouds of perfume and many more, remained fixed like clouds without dispersing. Cigarette smoke hung in one place and only gradually escaped. The jostle in the narrow streets was a burden, not an enjoyment to the stroller. The longer he walked, the more that disgusting condition took hold over him which is effected by the sea breeze and the scirocco and which is excitement and fatigue at the same time. He began to sweat unpleasantly. The eyes ceased to function, his chest felt tight, he was febrile, his pulse was pounding in his head. He fled from the business district to the quarters of the poor: there mendicants pursued him and the fetid stench from the canals made breathing even more difficult. In a quiet spot, one of those forgotten fairy tale places that can be found in the heart of Venice, resting next to a well, he dabbed dry his forehead and came to realize that he had to go somewhere else.

For the second time and permanently the city had proven to be very harmful to him in that kind of weather. Stubborn holding out seemed unreasonable, the probability of the wind changing direction was unknown. A quick decision had to be made. To return home already was not an option. Neither his summer nor winter quarters were ready for his arrival. But not only in Venice there were the sea and the beach, and in other places they could be found without the evil ingredients of the lagoon and its febrile effusion. He recalled a small seaside resort not far from Trieste, which had been praised. Why not go there? And that immediately, so that this change of location would still be worthwhile. He affirmed his decision and arose. At the next gondola landing he took a vehicle to convey him, through the dull labyrinth of the canals, below delicate marble balconies surrounded by lion sculptures, around slippery corners, along sorrowful palace facades with large company signs, which were mirrored in the garbage-topped water, to St Mark's. He had trouble getting there because the gondolier, who received payment from lace and glass manufacturers, tried to get him to do sightseeing and shopping and when the bizarre trip through Venice began to cast its spell, the mercenary spirit of the sunken queen contributed to an unpleasant sobering of the senses.

Back in the hotel he let the clerks in the office know that unforeseen circumstances required him to leave the very next morning. This was found regrettable, his bill was prepared. He had dinner and spent the balmy evening reading journals on the rear terrace. Before going to sleep he completely prepared his trunk for the next day.

He did not sleep very well as he was concerned about the impending departure. When he opened the window on the next morning the sky was still overcast but the air seemed refreshed, and—now his remorse began. Was this cancellation not hasty and in error, the conduct of an ill and unimportant state? Had he waited just a little more, had he made one more try to adapt to the Venetian atmosphere or considered the possibility that the weather might improve, then he could experience now, instead of haste and waste, a morning at the beach just like the day before. Too late. Now he had to continue wanting what he had wanted before. He got dressed and went down for breakfast at eight o'clock.

The buffet room was still deserted when he entered. Solitary figures appeared while he was waiting for what he had ordered. With the tea cup at his lips, he saw the Polish girls with their governess come into the room; austere and full of morning freshness, but with red eyes they paraded to their table in the corner. In the very next moment the porter approached and reminded him it was time to go. The car was waiting to transport him and other travelers to the Hotel "Excelsior" from where the motor launch would carry everyone through a private canal to the station. Time was pressing.—Aschenbach replied that time did not press at all. More than an hour remained until his train left. He did not like the habit of hotels to kick out their guests before their time and told the porter to let him finish his breakfast in peace. The man retreated hesitantly, only to reappear five minutes later. The car could wait no longer. Then he should drive away and take his luggage with him, Aschenbach responded angrily. He himself would, in due time, use the public steamer and would take care of his departure himself. The employee bowed. Aschenbach, relieved to have diverted the unwelcome exhortations, finished his meal unhurriedly, and even had the waiter bring him the daily newspaper. Time had grown quite short when he arose. It just so happened that Tadzio crossed the threshold that very moment.

Walking towards the table of his family, he crossed paths with Aschenbach, cast down his glance before the gray-haired man, only to look at him softly in his lovely way and passed. "Adieu, Tadzio!" thought Aschenbach. "It was all too brief." And as he, contrary to his usual habit, formed the words with his lips, he added: "God bless you!"—Next he organized his departure, gave tips, was bid farewell by the little soft-spoken manager in the French frock coat and left the hotel on foot as he had arrived to take the white-blossoming alley across the island to the steamship landing, followed by the manservant carrying his hand luggage. He reaches it, he takes a seat—and what followed was an odyssey through all shades of regret.

It was the familiar trip across the lagoon, passing St Mark's, up the Grand Canal. Aschenbach was seated on the circular bench at the bow, leaning with his arm upon the handrail, shading his eyes from the Sun. The municipal gardens retreated, the piazzetta opened out once more in princely charm and was left behind, next came the great row of palaces, and behind the bend of the waterway the magnificent arch of the Rialto Bridge appeared. The departing looked on, and his heart was torn. The atmosphere of the city, that slightly putrid smell which he had so sought to escape from—he breathed it now in deep, tenderly painful breaths. Was it possible that he did not know or had not taken into account how much he was attached to all of this? What had been a half-regretful, tiny doubt about the rightness of his decision now became a real pain, a desperation of the soul, so bitter that it brought tears to his eyes and of which he said to himself that he could not have foreseen it. What seemed to him so hard to bear, even intolerable, was apparently the notion that he would never again set eyes on Venice, that this would be a permanent farewell. Since it had been proven a second time that the city made him sick, as he had to leave it in a hurry again, he would have to consider it an impossible and forbidden place that was too much for him and where it made no sense to go back to. He even felt that, if he departed now, shame and defiance would keep him from ever seeing the city again, the demands of which on his body he had been unable to meet twice; and this discrepancy between his desire and physical potency suddenly appeared so grave and important to the senescent, the corporeal defeat so unacceptable and the need to prevent it at all costs so imperative, that he could not understand how he could have given in so easily and without a fight.

In the meantime the steamer approached the station and pain and perplexity increased until a state of confusion was reached. Departure seems impossible to the tormented soul, but so does staying. Absolutely torn that way he enters the station. It is already rather late, he has no time to lose if he wants to catch his train. He wants it and he wants it not. But time presses, it pushes him forward; he hastens to get his ticket and searches the jostle of the hall for the local officer of the hotel company. The man is found and reports that the large trunk has already been shipped. Already shipped? Yes, exactly—to Como. To Como? And after some heated discussion of irate questions and sheepish replies it emerges that the trunk, together with some other luggage, had been sent from the Hotel "Excelsior" into the completely wrong direction.

Aschenbach found it difficult to keep the expected expression on his face. An adventurous joy and unbelievable happiness moved him almost as in a fit. The employee ran off to possibly still hold the trunk back, but as surmised he returned unsuccessfully. So Aschenbach declared that he would not leave without his trunk but instead wanted to return to the Hotel des Bains to wait for it there. Was the motor launch of the society still at the station? The man affirmed that it was still there. He ordered the ticket clerk to take back the ticket, he swore to telegraph and that no expense would be spared to get back the trunk as soon as possible, and—so the odd thing took place that the traveler, twenty minutes after his arrival at the station, found himself again on the Grand Canal on his way back to the Lido.

Wondrously improbable, embarrassing, comically dreamlike experience: To see those places again within the hour from which one had tearfully departed forever, thanks to twists of fate! Foaming at the bow, maneuvering with dexterity between the gondolas and steamers, the fast little vehicle bolted towards its destination, while its passenger, under a mask of enraged resignation, hid the fearfully wanton attitude of a runaway boy. From time to time he was still moved to laughter about his misfortune that could not have been more timely. Explanations had to be given, surprised expressions had to be braved—and then all was well again, he said to himself, an accident had been prevented, a grave error corrected and everything he had believed to have left behind could be his again for as long as he desired... Did the speedy ride fool him or had the wind indeed turned and was now blowing from the sea?

The waves lapped against the concrete walls of the narrow canal, which leads across the island to the Hotel "Excelsior". A horseless omnibus was expecting the returning one and transported him on a road far above the undulating sea back to the Hotel des Bains. The little moustached manager came down the stairs to greet him.

Softly ingratiating he regretted the incident, called it very embarrassing for the hotel, but fully supported Aschenbach's decision to await the trunk here. Of course his room was already occupied, but a different one, no worse, would be available. *"Pas de chance, monsieur,"* said the Swiss elevator operator with a smile as they went up. And so the refugee took quarters again, in a room that was almost identical to first one in terms of the view and furnishings.

Weary and deadened from the chaos of that strange morning, he distributed the contents of his hand luggage in the room and sat down in an armchair next to the open window. The ocean had taken on a pale green color, the air seemed thinner and more pure, the beach with its boats and huts more colorful, even though the sky was still gray. Aschenbach looked outside, his hands folded in his lap, content to be back, shaking his head about his fickleness, his lack of knowledge about his own desires. So he sat maybe for an hour, resting and lost in mindless reverie. At noon he spotted Tadzio who, in a striped linen suit with a red bow, returned to the hotel via the wooden path. Aschenbach immediately recognized him, before he had even really looked at him, and wanted to think of something like: "Look, Tadzio, there you are again!" But in the same moment he felt the casual greeting sink and become silent in the face of the truth of his heart—felt the excitement of his blood, the joy and pain in his soul and realized that the farewell had been so taxing because of Tadzio.

He sat in utter silence, entirely unobserved on his high vantage point and looked inside of himself. The expression on his face had become enlivened, his eyebrows were moving up, an attentive, curious, and witty smile tensed his mouth. Then he raised his head and made with his arms, which had been hanging limply over the armrests of the chair, a slowly circular and raising motion, palms turned forward, as if suggesting an opening and extending of the arms. It was a willingly welcoming, calmly accepting gesture.

Chapter IV

From now on Helios drove his scorching chariot across the sky on every day, with his yellow curls blowing in the simultaneous Easterly breeze. Whitish-silky shine lay on the slowly undulating Pontus. The sand was scalding. Beneath the silvery-twinkling blue of the ether rust-colored canvases were stretching before the huts, and in the sharply delineated shadow they afforded one spent the morning hours. But the evening was also exquisite, when the vegetation in the park was spreading a balsamic scent, the celestial bodies above were advancing on their circles and the murmuring of the wine-dark sea, softly approaching, communed with one's soul. An evening like that guaranteed another sunny day full of joyful idleness and ornate with countless occasions for happy accidents in close proximity.

The guest who had been held here by just such a happy accident did not see any reason at all to depart as soon as he got back his trunk. For two days he had to endure some privation and could not dress for dinner otherwise than in his travel suit. Then, when one day the lost luggage was deposited in front of his room, he filled all the closets and drawers with his possessions, determined to stay for an indeterminate amount of time, and overjoyed at being able to spend his hours at the beach wearing his silk suit and looking presentable at dinner.

The pleasant regularity of this life had cast its spell on him, the soft and glowing mildness of this conduct had filled him with amazement. What a stay indeed, which combined the attractions of a civilized seaside life on a Southern beach with the cozy closeness of the wonderfully wondrous city! Aschenbach did not love pleasure. Whenever there was a party, a time to rest, to spend one's days with one's delights, he soon grew restless—and this had been particularly so in younger years—and demanded back the labor and sober service of his everyday life. Only this place could relax him, sooth his will, make him happy. Sometimes in the morning, dozing under his canvas, or in a balmy night, leaning against the soft gondola cushions, being ferried from St Mark's under a starry sky back to the Lido—with the garish lights and melodious sounds of the serenade receding—he recalled his house in the mountains, the location of his summertime duty, where the clouds moved through the garden, touching the ground, terrible thunderstorms made the lights in the house go extinct, and the ravens, fed by him, landed on the branches of firs. Then it appeared to him he was in Elysium, at the bounds of Earth where an easy life is granted people, where there is no snow nor winter nor storm nor deluge but always the softly-cooling breath of Oceanus and the days take their course in blissful idleness, without effort, without struggle, and completely devoted to the Sun and its feasts.

Often, almost constantly, Aschenbach saw the boy Tadzio; a limited space, a different order to everyone's life effected it that the arresting one was close to him most of the day, with short interruptions. He saw and met him everywhere: in the ground-floor rooms of the hotel, on the refreshing boat trips to the city and back, in the marvel of the square, and frequently in between on streets and paths if luck contributed. But mainly and with gratifying regularity the mornings at the beach gave him ample opportunity to study the beautiful figure devoutly. This predictability of happiness, these daily-recurring fortunate circumstances made the stay dearer to him and let every day seem like a Sunday.

He had risen early, as normally when he felt the drive to work, and was at the beach before everyone else, when the Sun was still mild and the sea lay blindingly white in morning dreams. He jovially greeted the man at the gate, also greeted the barefoot old man who had prepared his hut for him, deployed the canvas, and moved the furniture out onto the platform, and seated himself. The next three or four hours were his, in which the Sun ascended and gained fearsome power, in which the blue of the ocean deepened, and in which he could lay eyes upon Tadzio.

He saw him arrive from the left, close to the seashore, saw him come out backwards from between the huts, and sometimes found to his surprise that he had completely missed his entry and that he was already there, in that blue-white bathing suit that was his only dress at the beach, and had resumed his usual frolicking on the sunny sand—that sweetly inane, idly vagrant life, which was play and rest, an ambling, wading, digging, catching, reclining, and swimming, guarded by the women on the platform, who with soprano voices called for him: "Tadziu! Tadziu!" and whom he joined with eager gesturing, to tell them what he had experienced, to show them what he had found and caught: mussels, sea horses, jellyfish and crayfish that walked sideways. Aschenbach did not understand a single word of what he said, and it might have been the most everyday matter, it was still just gibberish to him. That way the foreignness of the boy turned speech into music, a wanton Sun bathed him in a prodigal splendor, and the majestic view of the distant sea always served as a backdrop to his figure.

Soon the onlooker knew every curve and pose of that sophisticated body that so freely exhibited itself, greeted again joyfully every already familiar pretty feature, and could find no end to his admiration and tender sensual pleasure. The boy was called to welcome a guest who was attending on the women at the hut; he came running thither, perhaps still dripping from the water, shook his curls, and, while extending his hand, standing on one leg while the other foot was on its toes, he had an appealing circular stance of the body, comely in a tense way, bashful because of his kindliness, eager to please out of aristocratic duty. He lay on the sand, his bath towel around his breast, his chin supported by his carefully chiseled arm; the one who was called "Jaschu" cowered next to him, cooing, and nothing could be more enchanting than the smile on eyes and lips with which the excellent one looked up at his inferior and servant. He stood at the shore, solitary and away from his people, very close to Aschenbach—erect, hands tied in his nape, slowly rocking back and forth on the balls of his feet, and dreamed into the blue, while small waves were washing over his toes. His honey-colored locks caressed his temples and the nape, the Sun illuminated the fluff of his upper spine, the finely drawn rips, the symmetry of the breasts was accentuated by his tight-fitting bathing suit, his armpits were still bare as in a statue, the hollows of his knees were shining, and their blue maze of veins made the entire body seem to be fashioned from some translucent substance. What discipline, what precision of thought found their expression in this elongated and youthfully perfect form! The severe and pure will that, working behind the scenes, had been able to bring this divine sculpture into being—was is not known to him, the artist? Did it not also work within him, when he, filled with prudent passion, coaxed that slender shape from the marble of the language that he had seen in his mind and which he put up before the people as an example and mirror of intellectual beauty?

Example and mirror! His eyes embraced that noble figure at the bounds of the blue, and in enthusiastic rapture he believed to embrace beauty itself, form as a thought in the mind of God, the one and pure perfection living in the human spirit and of which a human image and analog was erected here for worship. That was intoxication; and without hesitation, even eagerly, the artist welcomed it. His mind was flying, his learning surged up, his memory revived ancient notions from his youth that he had been taught but never thought about himself. Was it not written that the Sun shifted our attention from the intellectual to the corporeal? It confused and enchanted, it was said, the mind and the memory, so that the soul forgot its own disposition out of sheer joy and with stunned admiration attached itself to the most appealing of the lit objects: that it was then only able to reach higher spheres while beholding a body. Eros mimicked mathematicians who showed dull children concrete models of abstract shapes: That way also the god liked to use the form and color of human youth to make the conceptual visible, decorating it with all the reflections of beauty whose sight made us burn with pain and hope.

So ruminated the euphoric one; so were his feelings. And a delightful daydream out of the rumbling of the sea and the opulence of the Sun took shape before his eyes. It was the old plane-tree not far from the walls of Athens—that holy and shady place, filled with the scent of cherry trees, that was adorned with devotional images and pious gifts in honor of the nymphs and Achelous. A clear stream traversed smooth pebbles at the foot of the wide-branching tree; the crickets were chirping. On the soft-sloping grass two figures were reclining, protected from the heat of the day: an older and a younger one, one ugly and one winsome, the sage with the amiable. And with pleasantries and wittily wooing jests Socrates taught Phaedo about longing and virtue. He talked to him about the searing fright which is suffered by the one who beholds something that mirrors eternal beauty; talked to him about the cravings of the godless and evil one who cannot see the beauty behind its image and who is unable of reverence; talked about the holy terror that strikes the noble upon apparition of a perfect body before him, how he is shocked and does not dare to look at it, and how he would worship the one who is beautiful like a god if that did not make him look silly in the eyes of the others. Because only beauty, he added, is lovely and visible at the same time: it is, *nota bene*, the only way in which we can receive and bear the intellect. Or what would become of us when the divine in general, reason, virtue, and truth would be available like this to our senses? Would we not burn and die from love, like Semele before Zeus? Thus beauty is the way of the feeling one to reach the mind—only a *way*, a means, my little Phaedo... And then he landed his finest blow, the seasoned charmer: That the lover would be more divine than the beloved because God was in the former but not in the latter —perhaps the most tender and jocular notion ever conceived and the source of all waggishness and hidden wantonness of desire. The happiness of writers is the thought that can be entirely emotion and the emotion that can be entirely thought. Such a pulsing thought, such a precise emotion belonged to the solitary one then: namely that nature was shaken with delight when the mind paid homage to beauty. Suddenly he wanted to write. Eros loves idleness and is made for it, but in this stage of his condition the mind of the afflicted was set on production, the immediate cause was almost irrelevant. A question, an inspiration to make his position known about an important problem of culture and good taste had reached the traveler from the intellectual sphere. The subject was a familiar experience to him; his desire to see it take the glorious shape of words was unexpectedly irresistible. He wanted to work in the presence of Tadzio, to take the proportions of the boy as a template, to let his style flow like the curves of his body that seemed divine to him, to carry his beauty into the intellectual like the herder Ganymede had been lifted to the skies by the eagle-like Zeus. Never had the joy of words seemed sweeter to him, never had he been so conscious of Eros being *in* the words as in the dangerous and precious hours in which he, in full sight of his idol and under his canvas, worked on his little treatise—those one-and-a-half pages of exquisite prose, the honesty, nobility and emotional deepness of which caused it to be much admired within a short time. It is probably better that the world knows only the result, not the conditions under which it was achieved; because knowledge of the artist's sources of inspiration might bewilder them, drive them away and in that way nullify the effect of the excellent work. Strange hours! Strangely unnerving exertion! Strangely fertilizing intercourse between mind and body! When Aschenbach put aside his work and left the beach, he felt exhausted, shattered even, and it was as if his conscience was accusing him as if after a debauchery.

It was on the following morning that he, just leaving the hotel, saw Tadzio already on his way to the ocean—alone.

The wish to use this opportunity to meet and talk to the unknowing source of his emotional turmoil and inspiration, to enjoy his gaze and his replies seemed rather obvious. The beautiful one ambled leisurely, he could be overtaken and Aschenbach sped up his pace. He reaches him on the boardwalk behind the huts, he wants to place his hand upon his crown or shoulder and address him with a little phrase in French perhaps: there he feels that his heart is beating in his throat, maybe because of the brisk walking, that he is so out of breath that he will only be able to talk in a quivering voice; he hesitates, he tries to calm himself, suddenly he fears he has been walking behind him for too long, is afraid of him taking notice of that, tries a second time, fails, abstains, and passes with a lowered head.

Too late! he thought in that moment. Too late! But was it really too late? That step that he did not take might have led to good, light and happy things, might have cured him. Alone it seemed he did not want to be healed, that the intoxication was too dear to him. Who can make sense of the inward and outward manifestations of artists? Who can understand the deeply bonded alloy of order and intemperance that is its foundation? Because to refuse the sobering reality is intemperance. Aschenbach was no longer in a mood for being self-critical; the taste and mental state of his years, self-respect, maturity and late simplicity kept him from analyzing his motives and from deciding if he did not act because of his conscience or because of weakness. He was confused, he feared somebody might have witnessed his attack and subsequent defeat, he was afraid of ridicule. Otherwise he jested to himself about his comically holy terror. "Aghast like a cock who lets his wings hang limply in a fight," he thought. "That is truly a strange god who breaks our will and subdues our desire like that in the face of the amiable..." He played, raved, and was much to proud to be afraid of a feeling.

He finally stopped keeping track of the the grace period he had allowed himself; the thought of returning home did not even occur to him. He had obtained plenty of money through his writing. Only the possible departure of the Polish family concerned him; but he had learned en passant from the barber of the hotel that they had arrived immediately before himself. The Sun tanned his hands and face, the stimulating salty breeze strengthened him for emotions and whereas he usually spent all the refreshment given to him by slumber, food, and nature on his work, he now let all that which the Sun, idleness, and the marine air afforded him suffuse generously in intoxication and emotion.

His sleep was short; the deliciously uniform days were separated by brief nights of happy listlessness. He went to bed early, since the day seemed finished to him as soon as Tadzio had disappeared at around nine o'clock. But in the beginning dawn a tenderly penetrating fright awoke him, his heart remembered his adventure, he had to get up and so he did, and lightly clothed against the morning coolness he seated himself at the open window to expect the rising Sun. That wondrous event filled his soul, consecrated by the sleep, with devotion. The sky, the earth and the ocean were still lying in glassy paleness; a lone star was still twinkling in the nothingness. But a wind from forbidden distant places arose, for Eos to get up from the side of her husband and that first and sweet blush of the most remote parts of the sea and the skies happened, which portended the manifestation of creation. The boy-abducting goddess approached, who had robbed Cleitos and Cephalos and who had enjoyed the love of the handsome Orion, defying the other Olympians. A scattering of roses commenced at the bounds of the world, an unspeakably charming blossoming, infant clouds, blurry and translucent, were hovering like amoretti in the air in rosy-bluish scent, purple fell onto the sea which seemed to wash it ashore in undulations, golden spears came flying into the lofty sky, the brilliance became a burning, silently, with divine force the fervent flames ascended and with flying hoofs the brother's horse moved above Earth's circle. Blinded by the god's splendor the lonely one sat, he closed his eyes and let his eyelids be kissed by the Sun. Ancient feelings, early and delightful needs of his heart that had withered in the austere duty of his life and now returned miraculously transformed—he recognized them with a confused and bewildered smile. He was absorbed in thought and reverie, slowly his lips formed a name and still smiling and with his face turned upwards and his hands folded in his lap, he fell asleep in his chair again.

But the day which had begun so fiery and festal was strangely elevated and mythically metamorphosed in its entirety. Whence came that sudden breath which so softly caressed temple and ear like a divine whisper? Fluffy white clouds were standing in troops in the sky, like grazing herds of the gods. The current of air became stronger and Poseidon's horses where galloping along, also bulls belonging to the god, lowering their horns with a roar. Between the boulders of the more distant beach the waves jumped up like goats. A divinely disfigured world full of Pan's creatures surrounded the elated one, and his heart dreamed of tender fables. Several times, when the Sun set behind Venice, he sat on a bench in the park to watch Tadzio who, dressed in white and girded gaily, was playing ball on the flattened gravel court and it was Hyacinth he deemed to see who had to die because two gods fell in love with him. Yes, he felt Zephyr's painful jealousy of his rival Apollo, who neglected the Delphi oracle, the bow, and the cithara to play instead with his beloved; he saw the horrid discus hit the lovely head, he caught, turning pale as him, the limp body and the flower, sprung from that sweet blood, bore the inscription of his endless wail...

Nothing is more curious and awkward than the relationship of two people who only know each other with their eyes— who meet and observe each other daily, even hourly and who keep up the impression of disinterest either because of morals or because of a mental abnormality. Between them there is listlessness and pent-up curiosity, the hysteria of an unsatisfied, unnaturally suppressed need for communion and also a kind of tense respect. Because man loves and honors man as long as he is not able to judge him, and desire is a product of lacking knowledge.

Some kind of relationship or acquaintance had to come about between Aschenbach and Tadzio by necessity, and with penetrating joy the older one realized that concern and attention were not left entirely unanswered. What caused the beautiful lad, for example, to always enter the beach along Aschenbach's hut, across the sand and sometimes unnecessarily close to him, almost touching his table and chair, instead of taking the boardwalk behind the huts? Was this effected by the magnetism and fascination of a superior emotion on its tender and thoughtless object? Daily Aschenbach expected Tadzio's entry and sometimes he pretended to be occupied with something else when it happened and let him pass by apparently without taking notice. But at other times their gazes met. They were always deeply serious when that took place. Nothing in the educated and dignified expression of the older one betrayed an inner motion; but in Tadzio's eyes there was an inquiry, a pensive questioning, he hesitated in his walk, cast down his eyes, looked up again in a lovely way, and when he had passed, something in his attitude suggested that only good manners were keeping him from turning around.

But one evening it occurred differently. The Polish children with their governess had been absent during dinner in the large hall—Aschenbach had registered it with consternation. He took a walk after the meal, anxious about their whereabouts, in his dinner jacket and straw hat, at the foot of the terrace, when suddenly the nunlike sisters with the governess and four steps behind them Tadzio appeared in the light of the arc lights. Obviously they were coming from the steamship landing, after they had dined in the city for some reason. It had been chilly on the water; Tadzio was wearing a dark blue sailor's overcoat with golden buttons and an associated cap on his head. The Sun and the marine air did not burn him, his skin had stayed marble-like yellowish as in the beginning; but he seemed more pale than usual, be it because of the cold or because of the blanching moonlight of the lamps. His symmetrical brows looked more defined, his eyes very dark. He was more beautiful than can be expressed in words and Aschenbach again felt pain about the inability of words to truly describe beauty instead of just praising it.

He had not recognized the dear figure, it came unexpectedly, so he did not have time to take on an expression of calm and dignity. Joy, surprise, admiration could be read in it when his gaze met that of the missing one—and in that second it happened that Tadzio smiled: *smiled at him*, familiarly, lovely, and openly, with lips that only slowly parted during

61

the smile. It was the smile of Narcissus who bends above the reflecting water, that deep, enchanting, protracted smile, with which he extends his arms towards the mirror image of his own beauty—a slightly distorted smile, distorted from the hopelessness of his longing to kiss the pretty lips of his shadow, flirtatious, curious and somewhat tormented, infatuating and infatuated.

The addressee of that smile ran away with it as if with a calamitous gift. He was so moved that he was forced to flee the light of the terrace and the front garden and briskly made for the park on the rear side. Oddly indignant and affectionate admonitions escaped him: "You must never smile like that! Listen, you must never smile like that *at anyone!*" He threw himself onto a bench, frantically inhaling the nightly fragrance of the flora. And leaning back, with hanging arms, overcome and shivering, he whispered the formula of yearning—impossible here, absurd, depraved, ludicrous, and yet sacred and venerable even in this case: "I love you!"

Chapter V

In the fourth week of his stay on the Lido, Gustav von Aschenbach made some disconcerting observations regarding the external world. Firstly it seemed to him as if in spite of the approach of the best season the number of guests in his hotel was declining instead of increasing, and in particular as if the German language was dying out around him, so that during the meals and at the beach only foreign sounds could be heard after some time. One day at the barber's, whom he now visited regularly, he picked up a word that made him suspicious. The man had mentioned a German family which had left shortly after its arrival and added flatteringly: "But surely you will stay, sir; you are not afraid of the malady." Aschenbach looked at him. "The malady?" he repeated. The talker fell silent, tried to look busy, ignored the question, and when it was asked again more urgently he declared he did not know anything and tried to distract with embarrassed eloquence.

That had been at noon. In the afternoon Aschenbach crossed over to Venice during a calm and under a scorching Sun; since the obsession propelled him to follow the Polish siblings, whom he had seen take the path to the steamship landing accompanied by their governess. He did not find his idol at St Mark's. But when he took his tea at his little round iron table on the shaded portion of the square he suddenly noticed a strange aroma in the air, which it seemed he had registered subconsciously for a few days already—a sickly sweet smell reminiscent of distress and wounds and suspicious cleanliness. He probed it and pensively recognized it, finished his snack and exited the square on the side opposite of the church. In the cramped streets the odor intensified. At the corners printed notices had been affixed, warning the populace of the water in the canals and of the consumption of oysters and mussels, due to certain gastric conditions which had to be expected in this kind of weather. The euphemistic nature of the decree was apparent. Crowds of locals had gathered in silence on the bridges and squares; the foreigner stood brooding among them.

He attempted to get further information from a shopkeeper, who was leaning in the door of his store between coral necklaces and jewelry of artificial amethyst. The man assessed him with heavy eyes and rapidly enlivened: "Purely a precaution, dear sir," he said, gesticulating. "An order of the police that has to be observed. The weather is oppressive, the scirocco is not conducive to health. In short, you understand—likely an excessive precautionary measure..." Aschenbach thanked him and proceeded. On the steamer back to the Lido he also detected the scent of the disinfectant.

Back in the hotel, he immediately looked through the papers in the lobby. He found nothing in the foreign ones. The local papers reported rumors and fluctuating numbers, printed official announcements and questioned their veracity. This explained the withdrawal of the German and Austrian component. Members of the other nations were apparently ignorant of this, divined nothing, were unconcerned. "One should keep silent!" Aschenbach thought excitedly and threw the journals back onto their table. "One should keep silent about this!" But at the same time his heart filled with satisfaction about what the outside world was about to go through. Because passion, like crime, does not like everyday order and well-being and every slight undoing of the bourgeois system, every confusion and infestation of the world is welcome to it, because it can unconditionally expect to find its advantage in it. So Aschenbach felt a somber content about the cover-up of the terrible happenings in the grimy streets of the city that merged with his own innermost secret, happenings in the covertness of which he also had an interest. Because the lover was troubled by nothing except that Tadzio might depart and realized with terror that he would not know how to go on in life in that event.

As of late it was not enough for him to leave proximity and sight of the beautiful boy to chance or the daily schedule; he followed him around, he traced his steps. On Sunday for example the Poles never appeared at the beach; he guessed that they were attending Mass in St Mark's, he hastened there and entering from the fervent square into the golden dawn of the sanctuary, he found the needed one, praying during service. Then he stood in the back, on the jagged mosaic floor, among kneeling, murmuring people crossing themselves and the compact splendor of the Oriental-looking temple rested heavily on his senses. In the front, the ornate priest was singing and wielding his utensils, incense was in the air, encompassing the weak flames of the candles on the altar and into that dull and honeyed sacrificial scent another one seemed to mix: that of the sickened city. But through the mist and brilliance Aschenbach saw Tadzio turn his head, look for him, and find him.

When the crowds were exiting the church onto the gleaming square teeming with doves, the infatuated one hid himself in an ambush. He saw the Poles come from the church, saw the children say goodbye to their mother ceremoniously and how she turned to the piazzetta on her way back to the hotel; he determined that the handsome lad, his nunlike sisters and the governess were taking the way right of the clock tower and into the Merceria, and, putting some distance between them and himself, he followed them furtively on their walk through Venice.

He had to stop when they stopped, had to hide in cookshops and yards when they turned around; he lost sight of them, looked for them heatedly across bridges and in dirty blind alleys and had to suffer expressions of mortal pain when they suddenly came towards him in a narrow passage where evasion was impossible. Yet one could not say that he was suffering. His mind and his soul were intoxicated, and his steps were dictated by the demon who delights in destroying man's reason and dignity.

At some point, Tadzio and his took a gondola, and Aschenbach, hidden from their sight by a well, did the same when they had left. He talked in an abrupt and muffled voice when he ordered the gondolier, promising a hefty tip, to follow discreetly that gondola that was just turning the corner; and he was overjoyed when the man, with the roguish servility of the opportunist, replied to him in the same tone that he would be served, and served well.

So he floated, seated on soft black cushions, behind that other ebony barge, to which he was attracted by his passion. Sometimes he lost track of it: then he experienced grief and despair. But his gondolier, apparently experienced in such things, was always able to catch up with it by taking shortcuts. The air was calm and smelly, the Sun glowed through the haze, the sky was shale-colored. The waves clashed against wood and stone. The gondolier's call, partly warning, partly greeting, was replied to from somewhere in that silent labyrinth. White and purple umbels with an almond fragrance were hanging from high-lying gardens over derelict walls. Moorish window ornaments were dimly visible. The marble steps of a church descended into the water; a mendicant cowering on them presented his hat and showed the white of his eyes like a blind man, an antique dealer in front of his parlor invited the visitor with fawning gestures, hoping to swindle him. That was Venice, alluring and dubiously entrancing—this city, part fairy tale, part tourist trap, in the putrid atmosphere of which art used to blossom luxuriously and which had inspired musicians with lulling melodies. The adventurer felt as if his eyes were drinking that kind of luxury, as if his ears were courted by those kinds of melodies; he also recalled that the city was ailing and kept it secret because of its lucre, and he gazed even more unrestrainedly at the gondola in front.

So the confused one wished for nothing else except to pursue that object of his desire at all times, to dream of it in its absence, and, after the manner of lovers, speak tender words even to its shadow. Loneliness, foreignness, and the excitement of a late and deep rapture enticed him to allow himself to do even the most bizarre things without blushing or feeling shame, such as when he had, returning to the hotel in the evening, lingered before the beautiful boy's door on the second floor, pressing his brow against it and unable to part from it, risking to be caught in such an incriminating position.

But still there were moments of pause and contemplation. What kind of road! he thought. What kind of road have I chosen! Like every man who, because of his merits, takes an aristocratic interest in his ancestry, he was used to be in remembrance of his forefathers when he considered the achievements and successes of his life, to assure himself of their consent, their satisfaction, their necessary respect. He also remembered them at that moment, involved in such an unfit experience, taken in by such exotic emotional debauchery; he thought about their upright severity, the decent masculinity of their characters and smiled melancholically. What would they say about it? But really, what would they have said about his whole life, which had deviated so much from theirs, that life under the spell of art, about which he himself had once been so derisive as a youth, duplicating his forbearers' bourgeois attitudes, and that was yet in a way so similar to theirs! He also had served and exercised discipline; he had also been a soldier like some of them—because art was war, an exhausting struggle, in which one could only take part for a limited time these days. A life of overcoming oneself and yet a harsh, steady, and austere life, which he had turned into a symbol of a contemporary heroism—he was allowed to call it masculine and brave and it would seem to him that the kind of Eros, which had become his master, was particularly suited for such a life in some way. Was it not highly regarded among the most brave of peoples, was it not said that it blossomed in their cities through bravery? Countless war heroes of the past had been burdened with it, because nothing was considered debasing if it was ordered by the god, and deeds that would have been called acts of recreancy: falling to one's knees, oaths, imploring appeals and slavish devotion, these were not shameful for the lover but instead he was lauded for them.

That was the thinking of the infatuated one, in that way he tried to protect himself and keep his dignity. But at the same time he attentively observed the unclean going-ons in Venice, that adventure of the outside world which darkly converged with the one of his heart and nourished his passion with diffuse and lawless expectations. Bent on learning the latest about the current situation regarding the malady, he went through the local papers at the coffee houses of the city, because they had disappeared from the table in the hotel lobby. Claims and retractions were following each other. The number of cases and of deaths was supposed to be twenty, or forty, or a hundred, and right after that the whole notion of an epidemic was refuted, or at least limited to a few single cases of introduction from outside. Warning qualms, protests against the dangerous game of the officials were interspersed. Certainty was impossible to attain.

And still the loner was aware of a certain entitlement to learn the truth and, even though left out, he found it curiously satisfying to ask those in the know probing questions and force them to lie, since they had agreed to keep silent about it. One day at breakfast he did so with the manager, that little, soft-spoken man in the French frock coat, who was greeting and attending to the guests and also stopped at Aschenbach's table for a few words. Why in the name of God, inquired he in the most casual tone, had they been disinfecting Venice for some time?—"It is wholly a measure of the police, to keep all kinds of disruptions of public health in check that could be caused by the exceptionally hot weather."—"The police is to be commended," retorted Aschenbach, and after some exchange of meteorological remarks the manager took his leave.

On the same day, in the evening after dinner, it occurred that a small group of street musicians from the city was heard in the front garden. Two men and two women stood next to the iron post of an arc light with their brightly lit faces in the direction of the grand terrace, from which the vacationers enjoyed the folksy spectacle with coffee and cool drinks. The hotel employees, the elevator attendants, waiters and administrative office staff were listening from the entrance of the hall. The Russian family, eager and exact in matters of pleasure, had had chairs put up in the garden for them to be closer to the performers and sat there full of appreciation in a semicircle. Behind them, with her turban-like kerchief, stood their old servant.

A mandolin, a guitar, a harmonica and a scintillating fiddle were employed by the mendicant virtuosos. After instrumental pieces there were vocal numbers, such as the one where the younger woman, with a sharp and squawking voice, joined with the tenor in sweet falsetto for a love duet. But the main talent of the company was undoubtedly the man with the guitar and a sort of baritone-buffo, almost without a voice but with acting talent and possessing remarkable comedic energy. Often he separated from the group, his large instrument in his arm, coming up the ramp, where his fooling around was rewarded with cheering laughter. The Russians in particular were delighted with that southern agility and encouraged him with applause to become more and more sure of himself.

Aschenbach sat at the balustrade and sometimes wet his lips with a mixture of pomegranate juice and soda which glimmered ruby-red in his glass. He took in the squeaky music, the vulgar and pining melodies, because passion immobilizes good taste and seriously considers what soberly would be thought of as funny and to be resented. The clownish escapades had made him take on a fixed and almost hurting expression of amusement. He sat there in a relaxed way, while his interior was tense with attentiveness, because six paces apart from him Tadzio was leaning against the stone railing.

He stood there in a white suit which he sometimes wore for dinner, in inevitable and inborn grace, the left forearm on the railing, feet crossed, the right hand on his hip and looked with an expression that was almost unsmiling, more like a distant curiosity, a courteous acceptance at the singers below. Sometimes he straightened himself and pulled, with an elegant motion, his jacket through his leather belt. But at other times, and the older man registered it with triumph, with a floundering of his reason and also with horror, he turned around, either hesitatingly and slowly or quickly and suddenly, as if to take by surprise, over his left shoulder towards the chair of his lover. He did not meet his eyes, because a frightened concern forced the other one to keep himself from looking. Also on the terrace were the women who guarded Tadzio and he he feared to have become conspicuous. Indeed, he had noticed with a kind of torpidity that Tadzio had been called away from him, at the beach, in the hotel, and at St Mark's, that there was an attempt to keep them separate—and which implied a grave accusation which tormented him and which his conscience kept him from refuting.

In the meantime the guitarist had begun a solo to his own accompaniment, a multi-verse song that was currently making its rounds through Italy, in the refrain of which his company joined him with their singing and instruments and which he emphasized in a dramatic way. Lanky and with a thin and scrawny face he stood apart from the others, a sleazy felt in his nape, with a lump of his auburn hair protruding from under the brim, in an attitude of cheeky bravado on the gravel and emitted his jokes in a forceful recitative at the terrace to the tunes of his guitar, while the exertion of production made the veins on his forehead bulge. He did not look Venetian, rather like a Neapolitan comedian, part pimp, part gagman, brutal and bold, dangerous and entertaining. His normally relatively ridiculous song was transformed by his mouth and was made, thanks to his facial expressions, his body movements, his way of winking or salaciously playing with his tongue in the corners of his mouth, a little ambiguous and somehow objectionable. His skinny neck projected from the soft collar of his sport shirt, which he wore to his city clothes, exposing an unusually large and nude-looking Adam's apple. His pallid, round-nosed, beardless face, which made it difficult to guess his age, seemed ploughed up by grimacing and vice, and somehow the grinning of his nimble mouth did not fit the two deep furrows, defiant, imperious, and almost wild, between his reddish brows. But what really caused Aschenbach to focus on him was the observation that the suspicious figure seemed to carry with it its own suspicious ambience. Every time at the refrain, he started to dance around, shaking hands, coming close to Aschenbach's table, and every time that happened, his body and his clothes emanated a cloud of disinfectant smell.

After the song was finished, he started to collect the tips, beginning with the Russians, who were giving freely, and then made his way up the stairs. As cheeky as he had been during the song, as humbly he presented himself up here. Bowing, he tiptoed between the tables and a smile of sneaky servility bared his strong teeth, while the two furrows were still standing threateningly between his red brows. The alien being collecting his livelihood was examined with curiosity and some disgust, coins were thrown into his hat but people tried not to touch him. Closeness between the comedian and the decent audience always generates some awkwardness, even if the performance was very enjoyable. He felt it and tried to excuse himself with fawning. He approached Aschenbach and with him the scent which nobody else seemed to take note of.

"Listen," said the solitary one in a muffled voice, almost mechanically. "One is disinfecting Venice. Why?"—The comedian croaked: "Because of the police! It is an order, sir, in this heat and scirocco. The scirocco is oppressive. It is not conducive to health…" He talked as if he could not understand why one would ask about this and demonstrated with his flat palm how the scirocco was oppressive.—"So there is no malady in Venice?" Aschenbach asked softly and between his teeth.—The brawny features of the comedian took on a grimace of humorous perplexity. "A malady? What kind of malady? Is the scirocco a malady? Is our police a malady, perhaps? You must be joking! A malady! You must understand, it is purely a precautionary measure! A police order against the oppressive effects…" He gesticulated. —"It's all right," Aschenbach again said softly and quickly dropped a fairly large tip into his hat. Then he made a sign with his eyes for him to leave. The musician obeyed with a grin, under bows; but he had not yet reached the stairs when two hotel employees accosted him, taking him into a whispered cross examination. He shrugged, he pleaded, he swore to have been secretive; one agreed. Set free he returned to the garden and, after a hurried agreement with his company, broke into a final song.

It was a song which he foreigner thought never to have heard before; a cheeky song in unintelligible dialect and with a laughing refrain, into which the entire group entered at the top of their voices. Both the words and the musical accompaniment stopped at these points, and nothing remained except rhythmic laughter, which the soloist in particular performed with a remarkable verisimilitude. He had recovered his previous impudence, thanks to the increased distance to the audience and his faux laughter, addressed at the terrace, was derisive. Even before the refrain started he apparently had to fight the impulse. He sobbed, his voice wavered, he forced his hand against his mouth, he pulled up his shoulders, and in the right moment his laughter exploded, so real that it was infectious, so that the listeners became cheerful without a definite reason. And that seemed to increase the singer's giddiness. He flexed his knees, he slapped his thighs, he held his sides, he no longer laughed, he howled; he pointed with his finger at the merry society as if nothing could be funnier and finally everybody was laughing in the veranda and the garden, including the waiters, elevator attendants and servants in the door.

Aschenbach no longer reclined in his chair, he sat erect as if trying to fight or flee. But the laughter, the wafting hospital odor and the closeness of the beautiful boy immobilized him like an inescapable spell. In the general commotion and distraction he dared to look at Tadzio and registered that the other one also remained serious when answering his gaze, as if their behavior and expressions were linked and as if he was not influenced by the general mood since his lover was evading it. This childlike obedience was so disarming, so overpowering that the gray-haired one found it hard not to bury his face in his hands. It had also appeared to him that Tadzio's occasional straightenings and deep breaths were sighs, a tightness of the chest. "He is sickly, he will probably not reach old age," he thought with that objectivity to which intoxication and yearning are sometimes strangely inclined, and pure sympathy together with debauched satisfaction filled his heart.

The musicians meanwhile had finished and retreated. Applause accompanied them, and their leader did not fail to embellish his exit with jests. His bows and blowing of kissing were considered amusing, and so he redoubled them. When the others were already gone he pretended to run backwards into a lamp post, arriving at the gate in apparent pain. There he suddenly cast off his mask of the funny jinx, straightened himself up, stuck out his tongue at the guests on the terrace and disappeared into the darkness. The society of travelers dispersed; Tadzio was no longer standing at the balustrade. But the loner continued to sit with his drink at his table for a long time to the astonishment of the waiters. The night proceeded, time itself withered. In his parents' house, many years ago, there had been an hourglass—he suddenly saw the frail and important device again as if it stood before his eyes. Silently and finely the rust-colored sand traversed the glassy bottleneck, and since it was becoming less in the upper half, a small torrential vortex had formed there.

Already on the next day, in the afternoon, the defiant one made another attempt at tempting the outside world and this time very successfully. He entered the English travel agency at St Mark's Square and after he had exchanged some money, he addressed the clerk with his fatal question, with the expression of the distrustful stranger. It was an Englishman in tweed, still young, his hair parted down the middle, with narrow-set eyes, and that kind of loyalty of character which seems so alien and peculiar in the roguish South. He said: "No reason for concern, sir. A measure without grave implications. These kinds of orders are issued all the time to combat the ill effects of the heat and scirocco..." But looking up with his blue eyes he met the weary and somewhat sad gaze of the foreigner which was trained with slight disdain at his lips. The Englishman blushed. "That is," he continued, "the official version which people are trying to uphold. I will tell you there is something else to it..." And then he told the truth in his honest language.

For several years Indian cholera had shown an increased tendency to spread and travel. Born in the sultry swamps of the Ganges delta, ascended with the mephitic odor of that unrestrained and unfit wasteland, that wilderness avoided by men, in the bamboo thickets of which the tiger is crouching, the epidemic had spread to Hindustan, to China, to Afghanistan and Persia and even to Moscow. But while Europe was fearing the specter might make its entrance over land, it had appeared in several Mediterranean ports, spread by Syrian traders, had arrived in Toulon, Malaga, Palermo, and Naples, also in Calabria and Apulia. The North seemed to have been spared. But in May of that year, the horrible vibrios were discovered in the emaciated and blackened bodies of a sailor and of a greengrocer. The deaths were kept secret. But after a week it had been ten, twenty or thirty victims, and in different quarters. An Austrian man had died in his hometown under unambiguous circumstances, after he had vacationed for a few days in Venice and so the first rumors of the malady appeared in German newspapers. The officials of Venice responded that the public health situation had never been better and ordered the necessary measures to fight the disease. But the foodstuffs had probably been infected. Meat, vegetables and milk contributed to more deaths and the tepid water of the canals was particularly to blame. It seemed as if the disease had become more contagious and virulent. Cases of recovery were rare; eighty of a hundred infected persons died in the most horrible fashion, because the malady came in the particularly severe form called "dry cholera". Here the body was unable to even get rid of the water that came from the blood vessels. Within a few hours the afflicted person dried up and suffocated on his viscid blood amid spasms and croaky cries of pain. Comparatively lucky were those who, after a slight feeling of nauseousness fell into a deep blackout, from which they mostly did not come to again. In early June the quarantine barracks of the hospital had been filling silently, in the two orphanages there was no longer enough room, and a horrific traffic developed between the city and San Michele, the cemetery island. But the fear of general damage, regard for the recently opened exhibition of paintings in the municipal gardens, for the enormous financial losses that threatened the tourist industry in case of a panic, had more impact in the city than love of truth and observation of international agreements; it made feasible the official policy of secrecy and denial. The highest medical official had resigned, filled with indignation, and had been replaced with a more docile person. The people were aware of that; and the corruption at the top together with the reigning uncertainty, the state of emergency caused by the suffering all around, caused a certain demoralization, an encouragement of unsavory antisocial tendencies, which took form as debauchery, wantonness and a rise of criminal behavior. Against the normal rule, many drunken men were noticeable in the evenings; vile rabble made the streets unsafe in the night; robbery and even murder happened again and again, for two times it had already proven that supposed victims of the epidemic had in reality been killed by their relatives with poison; and prostitution became more obtrusive and excessive, in a way that was normally more associated with the South of the country or the Orient.

Finally the Englishman came to the most important thing. "You would be well advised," he concluded, "to leave today rather than tomorrow. The quarantine cannot be further away than a few days at best."—"I thank you," Aschenbach said and left the office.

The place lay in sunless sultriness. Ignorant foreigners were sitting in the cafés or stood, covered with doves, in front of the church and looked on as the birds, teeming, flapping their wings and shoving away each other, were picking the corn handed to them. In febrile excitement, triumphantly in possession of the truth, with a taste of disgust on his tongue and fantastic horror in heart, the loner paced up and down on the flags of the square. He considered a cathartic and decent deed. He could approach the pearl-wearing woman after dinner and talk to her like this: "Please allow this stranger, madam, to give you advice and warning, kept from you by selfishness. Depart, depart right now, with Tadzio and your daughters! Venice is diseased!" Then he could place his hand upon the crown of that tool of a taunting god, turn around and flee from this swamp. But he immediately felt he did not really want to take that step. It would lead him back, give his soul back to himself; but when one is frantic, the last thing one desires is to be oneself again. He recalled that white edifice, ornate with glistening inscriptions, in the iridescent mystery of which the mind wandered; that strange wanderer that had reawakened his youthful desire for distant places; and the thought of returning home, of prudence, of austerity, hardship and mastery seemed so repulsive to him that his face took on a grimace of bodily nauseousness. "One should keep silent!" he whispered impetuously. And: "I will keep silent!" The knowledge of his complicity intoxicated him, like a small amount of liquor intoxicates an old and faded brain. The image of the afflicted and derelict city caused him to hope for things that were unreasonable and of unspeakable sweetness. What was that little bit of happiness of which he had just dreamed in comparison to this? What was art and virtue to him compared to the advantages of disorder? He kept silent and stayed.

That night he had a terrible nightmare—if a mental and corporeal experience can be called that. It happened in deep sleep and complete independence and sensual presence, but without himself being part of the proceedings; the scene was his soul itself and the events intruded violently from outside, subduing his deep mental resistance, went through and left his existence, the culture of his life, in shambles.

Fear was the beginning, fear and lust and a horrified curiosity of what would be coming. It was night; and his senses were listening intently; because from away a commotion, a noise, a din approached: a rattling, a clashing, a muffled thunder, shrill cheers and a howling of an "oo" sound, all mixed and sweetly drowned in a terrible way with deep-sounding and continual flute-playing, which cast an obtrusive spell on the entrails. And he saw a phrase, dark, but denoting what was coming: "The alien God!" Smoky fervency was smoldering: there he recognized the mountains, similar to the ones surrounding his summer house. And in the spotty light, from woody hills, between trunks and mossy boulders it thundered earthward like a vortex: men, animals, a swarm, a raging horde and flooded the place with bodies, flames, tumult, and a lurching dance. Women, foundering over their long fur dresses hanging from their belts, were hitting tambourines above their heads, moaning, brandishing burning torches and naked daggers, holding hissing snakes or grabbing their bare breasts, crying. Men with horns on their heads, clad in furs and with hairy bodies, bent their necks and lifted arms and calfs, hit brazen cymbals and drums, while hairless boys were goading bucks, clasping their horns and letting themselves be carried away by their jumps with cheers. And the ecstatic crowd howled that soft cry with the stretched "oo" sound at the end, both sweet and wild: here it resounded like deer cries and there it was echoed, many-voiced, in wild triumph, inciting one another to dance and hurl the limbs and to never let the cry stop. But all that was ruled by the deep sound of the flute. Did it not also tempt him, reluctantly witnessing all this, with shameless perseverance to that feast and to the immoderate ultimate sacrifice? His abhorrence and his fear were big, his will was honorable, to defend what was his against that stranger, the enemy of the sober and dignified mind. But the din, the howling, multiplied by the rocky cliffs increased, became prevalent, swelling to a ravishing madness. Odors crowded the senses, the biting smell of the bucks, the scent of groaning bodies and the stench of putrid waters, also another familiar one: of wounds and sickness making its rounds. His heart was booming with the drumbeats, his brain was gyrating, anger gripped him, blindness, deadening sexual lust and his soul desired to join the god's dance. An enormous wooden phallus was uncovered: then they howled the password with even less restraint. With frothing lips they were clamoring, inciting each other with lusty gestures and straying hands, laughing and moaning—hitting each other with spiked rods and licking the blood from their limbs. And with them, obedient to their god Dionysus, was the dreamer. Indeed, they were *him*, when they killed the animals and ate the still tepid flesh raw, when they copulated on the mossy ground to honor their god. And his soul tasted fornication and the fury of downfall.

From these dreams the stricken one awakened, unnerved, shattered, and limply addicted to the demon. He no longer feared the watchful eye of the other people; their suspicion was no longer important to him. At any rate they were fleeing and departing; many beach huts stood empty, the dining room was not full, and in the city foreigners were only rarely seen. The truth seemed to have percolated and a panic unavoidable, despite the sticking-together of the interested parties. But the woman with the pearl necklace stayed, be it because the rumors did not get through to her or because she was too proud and unafraid to yield to them: Tadzio stayed; and Aschenbach sometimes thought that through departure or death everyone else could be removed so that he could remain alone with the beautiful boy on the island—when in the morning his looks rested heavily, irresponsibly, and continually on the desired one, when he followed him unworthily through he stinking streets with their air of death, this monstrosity seemed promising to him, and moral laws no longer applicable.

Like any other lover he wanted to please and feared this would be impossible. He added little embellishments to his suits to make them look more youthful, he wore jewelry and used perfume, multiple times a day he required a lot of time for his toilette, he was ornate, excited, and tense when he came to the dining room. In view of that sweet youth that infatuated him his worn-out body disgusted him, his gray hair, the sharp features of his face caused him to feel shame

81

and despair. He felt compelled to rejuvenate himself; he frequently visited the barber of the hotel.

In the hairdressing cape, under the grooming hands of the talkative barber, he looked at his mirror image with torment.

"Gray," he said with a distorted mouth.

"A little," said the man. "Because of a lack of care, an indifference to appearance, understandable in persons of importance, but that cannot be applauded and in particular since these kinds of persons should not be prejudiced with regards to what is real and what is artifice. If this sort of people rejected dental hygiene in the same way they reject cosmetics, they would leave a disturbing impression. After all we are only as old as our heart and mind feel and gray hair might be a greater falsehood than a little correction. You, dear sir, have a right to claim your natural hair color. Will you allow me to give it back to you?"

"How that?" asked Aschenbach.

Whereupon the talker rinsed the guest's hair with two solutions, a clear and a dark one, and it was as black as in his younger years. He curled it, stepped back and looked at his work.

"Only the facial skin would have to be refreshed a bit."

And like someone who is unable to stop himself he did one thing after another with zeal. Aschenbach, seated comfortably and unable to defend himself, hopeful about what transpired, saw in the mirror how his eyebrows arched upwards more elegantly, how his eyes looked larger and more shiny thanks to some makeup, saw his cheeks take on a rosy color, also his lips that had been pale were reddened, the furrows near eyes and mouth disappeared—he beheld with excitement an ephebe in full bloom. The cosmetician was finally content and thanked his patron after the custom of such people. "A minor correction," he said, putting the finishing touches on Aschenbach's exterior. "Now the gentleman can fall in love without hesitation." The enchanted one left, happy, confused, and fearful. His tie was red, his straw hat adorned with colorful bands.

A tepid breeze had started; it rained only occasionally and in small amounts, but the air was humid, thick and filled with putrid scents. Wafting, flapping and swishing filled one's ears and Aschenbach, feverish under his makeup, felt as if wind spirits of an evil kind were at work, like ugly sea birds digging into the condemned one's food. Because the sultriness stifled the appetite, and it was easy to think that the food was infected.

Following the handsome lad, Aschenbach had ventured deeply into the labyrinth of the afflicted city. Losing his orientation, since the little streets, canals, bridges and squares all looked too much alike, no longer sure about his bearing, he made an effort not to lose the desired idol from his sight and, forced into shameful delicacy, pressed against walls and taking cover behind other people, he did not realize how tired and exhausted his emotions and his suspense had made him. Tadzio was walking behind the others, letting the governess and his nunlike sisters go first in the cramped space, and ambling solitarily he sometimes turned his head, looking with his strangely gray eyes to make sure that his lover was still in tow. He saw him and did not give him away. Intoxicated by that knowledge, enticed to continue by those eyes, goaded by his passion, the inamorato traced an unsuitable hope—and still eventually had the sight taken away from him. The Poles had crossed a small, steeply curved bridge, the slope of which hid them and when he had ascended himself, he did not see them anymore. He searched for them in three different directions, straight ahead and both ways along the dirty and narrow quay, but to no avail. Feeling unnerved and weary, he had to abandon the hunt.

His head was burning, his body was covered with sticky sweat, his neck trembled, an unbearable thirst tormented him, he looked for some kind of immediate relief. He bought some fruit, some overripe strawberries, and devoured them while walking. A little square, looking deserted and enchanted, opened out before him, it had been here where he had planned to flee the city several weeks ago. He sat down next to the well, leaning against the stones. It was quiet, grass was sprouting between the slabs of the pavement. Debris was all around. Amid the derelict houses of uneven height at the square one stood out, like a palace, with pointed arch windows and little balconies with lions. There was also a pharmacy in the first floor of another house. Warm wind gusts sometimes carried with them the smell of disinfectant.

There he sat, the master, the dignified artist, the author of the "Miserable", who in such an exemplary and pure fashion had spoken against wandering and these murky depths, who had revoked his sympathy for the abyss and who had cast away what was cast away, the ascended one, the vanquisher of his knowledge and no longer partial to irony, who had accepted the responsibilities that fame brings, he whose fame was official, whose name bore the knighthood and who wrote in a style schoolboys were asked to imitate—he was sitting there, eyes closed, sometimes with a very fleeting expression of mockery and embarrassment and with his flaccid lips, improved through cosmetic artifice, forming occasional words out of what his half-sleeping brain was producing with a dreamlike logic.

"Because beauty, Phaedo, is the only thing that is divine and visible at the same time, and so it is the way of the artist to the soul. But do you believe, my dear Phaedo, that the one who reaches the intellectual through the senses can ever achieve wisdom and human dignity? Or do you believe (and I am leaving this to you) that it is a lovely but dangerous road that leads nowhere? Because you have to realize that we artists cannot take the path of beauty without Eros joining us and becoming our leader; we may be heroes in our own way, but we are still like women, because passion is what elevates us, and our desire is love—that is our lust and our disgrace. Do you see that poets can be neither sage nor dignified? That we always stray, adventurer in our emotions? The appearance of mastery in our style is a lie and foolishness, our fame a falsehood, the trust the public places in us is highly ridiculous, education of the young through art something that should be forbidden. Because how can someone be a good teacher when he has an inborn drive towards the abyss? We may deny it and gain dignity, but it still attracts us. We do not like final knowledge, because knowledge, Phaedo, has no dignity or severity: it knows, understands, forgives, without attitude; it is sympathetic to the abyss, it *is* the abyss. Therefore we deny it and instead seek beauty, simplicity, greatness and severity, of objectivity and form. But form and objectivity, Phaedo, lead the noble one to intoxication and desire, to horrible emotional transgressions rejected by his beautiful severity, lead to the abyss. Us poets, I say, it leads there, for we are unable to elevate ourselves, instead we can only transgress. And now I am leaving you, Phaedo; stay here until you no longer see me, then leave also."

*   *   *

A few days after that, Gustav von Aschenbach, feeling unwell, left the Hotel des Bains later than usual. He had struggled with certain fits of dizziness, only half physical, that were accompanied by strong feelings of fear and perplexity, a sense of hopelessness, of which it was not clear whether it pertained to the outside world or his own existence. In the lobby he saw a lot trunks and asked the porter who it was who was leaving and got as a reply an aristocratic Polish name of which he had already been dimly aware. His decayed features did not change when he heard it, he made a tiny gesture with his head as if it was something not worth knowing about and inquired: "When?" The response was: "After lunch." He nodded and went out towards the ocean.

It was unwelcoming there. Undulating ripples ran across the distant sea between the beach and the first sandbank. A sense of autumn lay over the place that had once been so lively and colorful, that was now almost abandoned and the beach of which was no longer kept clean. A camera, apparently unappropriated, stood at the shore on a tripod and the black cloth that was draped over it was flapping in the cold breeze.

Tadzio was playing at the right in front of their hut with the three or four comrades he had left and Aschenbach watched him for a last time, with a blanket on his knees, seated about midway between the sea and the row of huts. The game, that was unsupervised, as the women were probably busy with the impending departure, seemed to be without rules and soon degenerated. The sturdy one called "Jaschu" had been blinded by a throw of sand towards his eyes and had forced Tadzio to wrestle, a fight that quickly ended with the beautiful but weaker one's defeat. But as if in the hour of departure his servile attitude had become brutal and wanted to avenge itself for that long slavery, the victor kneeled on Tadzio's back and forced his head into the sand, so that Tadzio could have suffocated. His attempts to throw off the boy on his back slowly subsided. The horrified Aschenbach almost wanted to step in when the victim was finally released. Tadzio, very pale, sat up and remained there for a few minutes unmoving and with dark eyes and disorderly hair. Then he stood up and went away. He was called, at first heartily, then imploringly; but he did not respond. The black-haired one, who might have felt regret about his transgression, overtook him and tried to reconcile himself with him. A gesture of the shoulder rebuked him. Tadzio walked diagonally towards the water. He was barefoot and wore his striped bathing suit with the red bow.

At the edge of the water he remained, drawing figures into the sand with his toes, his gaze fixed at the ground. Then he crossed the shallow sea that reached up to his knees in its deepest parts and arrived at the sandbank. There he stood for a moment, looking into the distance and then wandered slowly towards the left. Separated from terra firma by a gulf of water, separated from his companions by his pride, he ambled as a distinct and unconnected figure in the sea, in the wind, before the misty boundless space. Again he stood still to gaze. And suddenly, as if remembering something, he turned his torso, one hand at his side and looked over his shoulder to the shore. The onlooker sat there as he had when their eyes had first met. His eyes had been trained on the stroller, his head leaning against the chair, but now his head rose to meet the glance and then sunk back onto his chest as if in a deep sleep. But to him it seemed as if that pale and lovely Hermes out there was smiling at him, beckoning him; as if he, taking his hand from his side, was pointing at and floating into that promising immensity. And as he was used to do, Aschenbach followed him.

Several minutes passed before help arrived for him, who had fallen over sideways in his chair. He was carried to his room. And on the very same day a respectfully shocked world received the news of his death.

TRANSLATED BY MARTIN C. DOEGE